THE GINGERBREAD WITCH

**Books by Alexandra Overy
available from Inkyard Press**

Middle Grade

The Gingerbread Witch

Young Adult

These Feathered Flames
This Cursed Crown

THE GINGERBREAD WITCH

ALEXANDRA OVERY

ISBN-13: 978-1-335-42686-4

The Gingerbread Witch

For questions and comments about the quality of this book, please contact us at CustomerService@Harlequin.com.

Inkyard Press
22 Adelaide St. West, 41st Floor
Toronto, Ontario M5H 4E3, Canada
www.InkyardPress.com

Printed in U.S.A.

For my grandparents Barbara and Ken,
who were the first to show me the magic of fairy tales.

WHERE THE BONES SING

EVERWOOD

GLASSFALL

GOBBLEHIVE

THE WARBLING BROOK

AGATHA'S COTTAGE

THE GLASS COFFIN

SEVEN RAVEN HILL

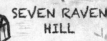

APPLE'S BITE

THE DRAGON'S LIBRARY

THREE SPINNERS' GROVE

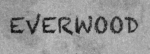

MERLAKE

THE FROG
KING'S THRONE

← POISON
LOCH

DIGGERING
SWAMP

WHERE THE
STARS MEET

UNREACHED
TOWER

THUMBLING

THE
ABANDONED
FOREST

GONE

THE
SHADELANDS

← THE
WANDERING
TREE

Common
Spells for
Uncommon
Witchery

1
TALONS
OR TOENAILS

On her eleventh birthday, Maud asked for spellcasting lessons. She'd read enough stories to know that was when most young witches came of age, and it was the ideal time to start nurturing her gift. Mother Agatha had been less convinced. But after Maud's incessant nagging, she'd relented that, *one day*, she would teach her.

Well, Maud's twelfth birthday had come and gone, and it was becoming increasingly clear that *one day* really meant *never*.

So Maud was taking matters into her own hands.

"This is a terrible idea."

Maud laid the heavy, leather-bound book out on the table. "You're only saying that because you didn't think of it first."

The squirrel hopped after her. "No, I'm saying it because *it's a bad idea*."

Maud ran her fingers over the soft leather of the cover, tracing the title, *Common Spells for Uncommon Witchery*. "You know," she said with a glance at Nuss. "This is why Grim's my favorite. He doesn't criticize my ideas."

The three-legged wolf cocked his head at the sound of his name, looking up from his spot in front of the fireplace. With his razor-sharp teeth and massive paws, Grim could have looked intimidating. A ferocious familiar for any powerful witch. But Grim had a tendency to sit with his tongue sticking out, which, combined with the pale violet hue of his fur, somewhat ruined his intimidation factor.

Nuss shot Maud a glare, flicking her hazelnut-mousse tail so that it sent flecks of cream flying. "Grim can't talk."

"Careful," Maud snapped. "Mother Agatha will know I had the book down if you get that on it."

"Mother Agatha will know anyway," Nuss grumbled.

Usually, Nuss would be right. Mother Agatha had a way

of sensing mischievous ideas before they'd even fully formed in Maud's head.

But today, Agatha would be gone until sundown. She didn't usually leave Maud alone for so long, but she had a lead on some fresh nightshade apples that she couldn't turn down. Agatha claimed they made the best apple pie east of the frozen river—better than the Butterfly Witch's famous poison apple pie. Agatha had even taken Florian with her to better keep track of the trail, so there were no vulture eyes watching over Maud.

While Maud might feel a little guilty for taking advantage of that—especially when she'd been promised said apple pie if she was good—the excitement of the spellbook eclipsed it. It was a forbidden thing. Wonder and magic and possibilities all bound in paper.

And she was finally holding it.

"Mother Agatha won't know," she said, partly to convince herself. "Not if no one tells her, anyway." She narrowed her eyes at the squirrel in accusation.

Nuss drew herself up to her fullest—and not-at-all-impressive—height. "I will have you know that *I* am no snitch. I simply want it on the record that I said this was a bad idea from the start."

Maud waved a hand in her direction. "It's better than no idea." It was better than sitting around doing nothing when all this magic was right in front of her, begging to be tested.

The squirrel let out a chirruping sigh. "But you don't know any spells. Where would you even start?"

Nuss did have a point. There were so many possibilities in this kitchen that it was a little overwhelming.

You see, Mother Agatha's kitchen was not like most kitchens. For one, right next to the neatly labeled containers of sugar, flour, cinnamon, and the like sat more…*unusual* ingredients. A jar of pale, unseeing salamander eyes. Piles of dried snakeskin and dragon scales nestled next to a glass jar filled with small white objects that looked suspiciously like baby teeth.

But the ingredients were not what made Mother Agatha's kitchen remarkable. In fact, it was common practice for any self-respecting witch to have various dismembered body parts on hand. No, what made the room undeniably strange—even by witch standards—was that it was made entirely of sweets.

At first glance, the sturdy table may appear to be made of oak, but a careful observer would notice the finely carved piece was actually hewn from gingerbread. The windowpanes were melted sugar, embellished with bright lemon drops and spun-sugar curtains. The ticking cuckoo clock above the mantel was comprised of buttery short-bread panels, held together by richest caramel. Even the logs in the fireplace were molded from chocolate.

But Maud was used to all of that; she wouldn't let it stop her. She just had to start small.

"I know spells," Maud said to Nuss, a little indignant. "Well, I've seen Mother Agatha do spells. I've helped her prepare the ingredients. That's pretty much the same."

It most definitely wasn't *pretty much the same,* but Maud didn't want to admit that. There was a small, vulture-shaped voice in the back of her head that very much agreed with Nuss. This probably was a terrible idea.

But it was also her only chance. If she could do this spell, if she could get it to work, then Mother Agatha would have to agree to teach her. She'd have to.

Maud flicked through the pages and settled on one she recognized. Firestarter. The spell to create the small magical flames witches used for their cauldrons. The first spell any young witch should know—or so Maud guessed. After all, without a cauldron flame, she couldn't do much else.

Agatha had several prepared powders for when she needed cauldron flames. An experienced witch could use just a dash of it. They connected their minds to the components and, *poof*, flame. But for a novice like Maud, she needed the physical connection of ingredients and a spell.

She ran her finger down the page. Each recipe was written out in a neat block script, with small annotations in Agatha's cramped hand. Incantations to help bottle moonlight, spells to crystalize a memory, enchantments for eternal slumber, charms to keep away nosy children. They went on and on, all these amazing possibilities.

Maud's finger stopped at one that didn't have too many steps.

"A purple flame sounds easy enough."

She didn't wait for Nuss's protests. Turning to Agatha's vast wall of jars and pots, Maud scanned for the first ingredient—dryad ashes, the basic link to the earth. She spotted a small brass urn, neatly labeled, and grabbed it.

"Okay," she murmured, turning back to the list. "So, I still need dragon toenails for the strength to hold it together, goblin entrails for a spark, pond water bubbles for air… and essence of eye of newt for concentration."

Maud reached for a flask labeled *Pond Water Bub-*

bles from the Diggering Swamp, sending two sugar mice squealing back into their house as she dislodged their hiding place. She just managed to reach the glass jar of goblin entrails on her tiptoes and swiped the small dropper of eye of newt, but the last ingredient proved to be tricky.

"Can you get the dragon toenails for me?" she asked Nuss, gesturing to the highest shelf.

"Why do I have to?"

Maud rolled her eyes at the obvious question. "Because I can't reach up there."

Nuss let out a dramatic sigh—but Maud knew she wanted to be involved. If there was rule breaking to be done, the squirrel *always* wanted to be involved. And now that she'd established she had the right to say "I told you so" if this went wrong, Nuss seemed far more invested in the proceedings.

The squirrel leaped up the gingerbread shelves with ease, sending a spatter of crumbs down in her wake. She scurried along the top, sniffing each bottle and jar.

"Wait, dragon talons or dragon toenails?" Nuss called down.

Maud chewed her lip. "Is there a difference? Do dragons even have toenails?"

"Well, we only have talons," the squirrel said from her perch on the shelf. "So those'll have to do."

She hopped back down—small pot of silvery powder in paw—and nearly knocked over the sky serpent venom in her excitement. Maud only just managed to catch the jar before it hit the ground. The last thing she needed was a mess to let Mother Agatha know what she'd been up to.

Putting the ingredients together was the easy part. All Maud had to do was follow the instructions, just like any other recipe. Start with a pinch of the ashes, a sliver of entrails, a dash of pond bubbles, and then the dragon talons followed by a single drop of eye of newt. Maud had watched Agatha do it a thousand times—she'd even helped with some of the steps herself.

But this last step, this was the true test.

Even if Maud refused to admit it, her stomach was churning at the thought.

She'd never read the language of magic before. She'd heard Agatha recite it, of course, but that wasn't the same, and Maud had never been allowed close enough to the book to try reading it herself. It was supposed to be instinctive. It required proper training to get it perfect, but young witches should be able to work out the most basic parts on their own.

She stared down at the incantation written at the bottom of the page. The symbols seemed to shift before her eyes the longer she looked at them, swirling away like smoke on the wind. She dug her nails into the chocolate countertop, concentrating. But no matter how much she glared at the incantation, it remained stubbornly illegible.

Nuss nudged her arm gently. "You might not be able to read it."

"No," Maud said, more forcefully than she'd intended. "I have a witchmark. I'm a witch." *I have to be*, she added inside her head. Because if she wasn't a witch, then what was she? A piece of gingerbread Agatha had enchanted on a whim?

Because, though Maud may look like any other child, she was not.

Just like Agatha's other creations before her—Florian, Nuss, even the cottage itself—Maud had been made from gingerbread. Unlike the other creatures, though, magic had crafted Maud into something that resembled flesh and blood, something that could grow and change beyond its gingerbread core. While the others still had the look of sweet creations, with hazelnut-mousse fur or sugar-spun feathers, Maud's short black hair and dark eyes looked as real as any human's.

She even had the pale outline of a witchmark on the white skin of her wrist, the crescent-moon mark that appeared on all young witches.

But that didn't change what she'd come from. It didn't change that, in her heart, she was nothing more than crumbs.

She shook her head. No, she was definitely more than that. And this would prove it.

She glanced back at the spell. Maybe she was trying too hard. This was meant to be natural, wasn't it?

Letting her eyes slide out of focus, she looked back down at the incantation. For an instant, the swirling letters coalesced into something else. Not like letters in a normal book—but something Maud understood. *Instinctively.*

Excitement fizzed in her chest. She shook her head, unfocusing her gaze again. The spell slipped into meaning once more, like she'd brushed back a layer of frost from the sugared windowpanes.

She held one hand over the small cauldron of ingredients and took a steadying breath.

"Em rof thgirb ezalb."

The words felt rough on her tongue, leaving a gritty aftertaste as if she'd swallowed dirt. She wasn't sure if that was a bad sign or not.

At first, nothing happened. Nuss let out a low chitter.

Then, for just a heartbeat, Maud felt it. A trickle of magic, as right as the blood that flowed in her veins. A brief burst of sunlight through the clouds on a gray day.

And then it exploded.

Not exploded in the way a soufflé sometimes exploded if you opened the oven door too soon—a small poof and a sad drizzle of chocolate. No, this explosion was more like she'd dropped fireworks in a vat of caramel. Or perhaps like a tornado had decided to try its hand at whipping meringue.

Maud blinked goo from her eyes. She was drenched. Debris rained down around her, purplish slime covering every surface. A jar of banshee screams shattered against the floor, letting out a high-pitched wail that made Maud cover her ears. Even Nuss was buried under what looked like a fallen jar of ghost eyeballs.

Maud had no idea how such a small cauldron could make this much mess.

Luck was really not on Maud's side today, because it was at that precise moment that Mother Agatha opened the door.

2
AN UNEXPECTED VISITOR

Two hours later, Maud was still scrubbing goblin guts from the wall. Mother Agatha *could* have cleaned the whole thing up in less than a few seconds with a scouring spell, but apparently Maud wouldn't learn her lesson that way.

"Make sure you put as much of that back in the jar as you can, sweetest," Mother Agatha said, taking a sip of her frog scale tea. "Goblin entrails are hard to come by this time of year."

Maud let out an irritated huff, letting more of the entrails splatter down the side of the jar.

Florian's sharp eyes watched from his perch in the corner, his buttercream ruff still quivering with indignance. Mother Agatha had at least given up on her lecture after an hour, but the vulture was relentless.

"Honestly," Florian said for the fiftieth time, accompanied with his signature long-suffering sigh. "You don't even know the difference between a talon and a toenail."

"I know the difference," Maud said. She scrubbed at a particularly stubborn spot of purple gunk. "I just think there could be an argument made for them being the same thing."

He swept a wing toward the mess. "Evidently not."

Florian had long since perfected his arched look of disapproval, complete with a single raised eyebrow that Maud was secretly jealous of. Well, not quite a raised *eyebrow* but whatever the equivalent was for a vulture.

"Perhaps if someone would teach me the difference…" Maud said with a pointed look at Mother Agatha.

Agatha stirred her tea. "I've told you before, the time isn't right," she said. "Especially when you take it upon yourself to use my spellbook without asking permission."

Maud threw the rag onto the floor, glaring up at Agatha. "I don't see what's so wrong with trying to learn.

You wouldn't teach me, so I came up with a solution." She rolled up her left sleeve, pointing to the crescent moon that shone on her forearm like a scar. "I have a witchmark. And I know the spell went wrong, but I felt magic. I'm sure I did." She turned to Nuss. "You saw it, didn't you?"

The squirrel let out a nervous chitter. "I was a bit too busy getting covered in slime to see anything."

Maud stood up, squaring her shoulders to face Mother Agatha again. She wasn't giving up, not this time. "I know I can do magic."

Agatha let out a heavy sigh. "Just because you can doesn't always mean you *should*, sweetest."

"What does that mean?"

Maud had a bad feeling she was about to be told something she wouldn't like. It festered in her stomach like spoiled milk, and suddenly, she wanted to run out into the frost-covered woods before Mother Agatha could say anything else.

"You're young," Agatha said, in a frustratingly calm voice. "There are things I can't explain yet, but—"

"Other witches my age have already joined the Witching Guild. The Goblin Witch's apprentice joined when she was *ten*," Maud pressed. "They aren't too young to learn."

Agatha's expression was too gentle. "But you're not like other children your age."

Maud swallowed. A familiar fear rose in her chest. That bitter reminder that, even if she looked human, she most definitely wasn't.

"Why does that matter?" She'd meant her voice to come out defiant, but it sounded more like a sugar mouse's scared squeak.

But Mother Agatha didn't reply. Her head snapped toward the doorway as if she'd heard a sound. She rose to her feet, the color draining from her face. "Someone's here."

Maud followed her gaze, confused. She couldn't hear footsteps, and there was no sign of a shadow against the window. Besides, no one ever came to the cottage. It was protected against unwanted visitors or wandering children.

But Mother Agatha sounded so certain.

Maud went to look out the window, but Agatha's arm held her back. "No," she said, her voice suddenly sharp.

"Who is it?" Maud asked, trying to twist out of her grip.

But, though Mother Agatha may appear old and frail, her strength was that of a baker. She led Maud firmly to-

24

ward the back door and held out a woven basket. "Go pick some frostberries for the eclairs."

"But I want to see the visitor—"

"Maud," Agatha said, in that special voice of hers that meant there would be no arguing with her. "Go get the frostberries."

Maud snatched the basket from her with a glower. "That's all you ever say. Go fetch this. Go whisk that." She clenched her fist, her frustration bubbling over like an unwatched cauldron. "I don't know why you even made me if you didn't want me to be a part of anything."

It was the question that always burned inside her, just out of reach. The question of why Mother Agatha had created her. Why she'd gone to all those lengths to transform gingerbread into flesh and blood.

But now that she'd asked, Maud wasn't sure she wanted to hear the answer. So instead, she marched out the back door, Grim trotting at her heels and goblin entrails squelching in her wake. If Agatha didn't want her around, then she wouldn't *be* around. Maud ran to the low wall that rimmed the cottage, a patchwork of rainbow gumdrops that formed the protection spell.

She kicked at it. She'd hoped it might make her feel a bit better, but all it did was leave her with a sore toe.

She was so preoccupied with her annoyance as she ran toward the wood, she didn't even notice that her kick had done more than make her big toe throb. It had also broken off a small shard of gumdrop—a small piece of the spell that protected the cottage.

3
A WOLF
AT THE DOOR

Maud sat on a fallen log, scuffing the powdered-sugar dusting of snow at her feet. Her basket lay abandoned a few paces away. Grim nosed about, hoping for something more appetizing than the icy mud of the forest.

Maud wasn't sure how long she'd been sitting there, but twilight was creeping over the treetops. She hoped it was long enough that Mother Agatha was beginning to worry. That'd make her sorry she'd sent Maud on an errand rather than let her meet the visitor. Rather than let her do *anything* interesting.

But the downside was that the log wasn't very interesting either. And with the frost still clinging to the branches, she was already shivering.

She glanced over at Grim. "You think I'm right, don't you?"

As usual, Grim didn't reply. He might live in the gingerbread cottage, but he wasn't one of Agatha's creations. Last winter, Agatha had found him wondering alone in the wood, abandoned because, with only three legs, he couldn't keep up with the pack. She'd taken him in, entrusting his care to Maud.

Maud had hoped it meant the first step in her witchery training—getting a familiar was vital for any young witch—but she'd been wrong about that too.

She folded her arms. "If Agatha really wants me back, she'll come find me."

Grim nudged her leg and she glanced down at him.

"I know it's cold," she said. "And we're not meant to be in the woods after dark. But I'm making a stand." She shifted on the log. "A sitting stand."

She snuck a sidelong glance at the wolf pup. He looked up at her with his big, shimmering eyes.

She let out a sigh. "I know, I know. I should go back."

Despite not talking, Grim gave good advice.

With another sigh, she picked up the basket and began to make her way back through the trees. She half-heartedly picked a few frostberries she saw along the way so she'd at least have something to show for herself.

But with her anger at Agatha fading away, she was left with an odd feeling in her stomach. The fear that some-times crept in when Maud was trying to sleep. What if Agatha really had made her on a whim, for no reason at all? What if she was just another experiment? Maybe Agatha had wanted to see how far she could press the magical properties of gingerbread, testing its ability to hold life, nothing grander than that.

Maud shook her head, grabbing another bunch of frost-berries. With the sky turning dark, the shadows of the for-est reached toward her. Suddenly, she wanted nothing more than to be back in the cottage, sitting by the warm fire as Florian admonished her for staying out so late.

Grim bounded ahead, and she hurried after, following his path through the snow until she reached the edge of the clearing.

As soon as Maud stepped out of the trees, she knew something was wrong.

There was nothing out of place—the strawberry-pink

front door sat closed; lilac smoke still puffed from the chimney—but there was an odd prickling on the back of her neck. She paused, Grim nudging at her knees.

A shadow flickered in the cottage window, and Maud's heart leaped into her throat. That wasn't an Agatha-shaped shadow. It wasn't a flutter of wings or a swishing tail.

Maud took a tentative step forward. The shadow shifted, turning away from the window, and Maud caught a glint of silver.

It couldn't be—

Her feet were moving before her brain had even comprehended what she'd seen. She sprinted toward the cottage, stumbling over stubborn patches of ice and stray rocks. Jumping over the gumdrop wall, she skidded to a stop under one of the sugared windows.

Heart hammering, she peered over the ledge. Two people stood in front of the huge stone oven. They wore matching silver cloaks, and matching swords hung at their waists, the hilts curled over to look like a wolf's claws. One was slightly taller, with a crop of sandy hair just peeking out from his hood, and the other had their hood down to reveal dark brown plaits.

They didn't look much older than Maud herself.

But their masks were unmistakable. Sharp silver ears, gleaming fangs in an open snarl.

Wolves.

But Wolves weren't meant to be real. They were a distant story that young witches whispered after dark, spinning tales of the mythical witch hunters to scare their friends. They belonged in books—the ones Maud wasn't meant to read yet but snuck away with anyway.

They *definitely* didn't belong in Agatha's kitchen.

The taller of the two shifted his feet, and his voice drifted out to where Maud crouched. "I don't know what we do next, all right? It's complicated."

The girl scoffed. "Okay then, Mr. I'm-so-brilliant-I-have-the-handbook-memorized."

"The handbook doesn't exactly cover this."

The boy turned, and Maud ducked out of sight. She pressed against the crumbly gingerbread of the wall, hoping he hadn't seen her. When no shouts came, no running feet, she let out a low breath.

Her thoughts were whirling. What in all the Old Witches' names were Wolves doing in the cottage? Surely they couldn't have been the visitor from earlier, so how did they get in?

But one question whispered behind all the others, too worrying to voice: Where was Agatha?

Maud's eyes skimmed over the garden and the trees beyond. Maybe Agatha had gone searching for her in the wood? But Maud couldn't see any hint of movement beyond the garden, and Agatha's fruit-leather Wellington boots still sat by the gate. She'd hardly have gone out into the woods in her slippers.

That was when Maud noticed. A dark crack ran down the rainbow-hued wall that ringed the cottage. One of the gumdrops lay crooked and out of place, exactly where she'd kicked it only hours before.

She gasped. She'd broken the protection spell and made the cottage visible to outsiders. *That* was how the Wolves had found them. How could she have been so stupid?

She'd stormed off, and now there were Wolves in the cottage, and she couldn't find Agatha or any of the others, and—

Maud closed her eyes. Agatha's voice echoed in her mind: *you can't see the way forward if your head's spinning*

she'd never done it with her blood pounding like a drum and Wolves snapping at her heels.

She reached for the first branch and pulled herself up. An apple glimmered just above her head, encased in a golden layer of caramel. She grabbed it, tucking it beneath her arm as she slid back down.

The bark scraped against her palms, but she ignored it. She had to get to that wall. She reached for a foothold when the voices, suddenly louder, made her jump.

"I say we just burn it all down and go home."

The boy sighed. "Why is your answer always pyrotechnics?"

Distracted, Maud's foot missed the knot, and she crashed to the ground.

"There's someone out there!" one of the voices yelled.

Maud scrambled to her feet. Her heart pounded in her ears, so loud she almost didn't hear the Wolves' shouts.

She leaped over the path, nearly stumbling again as her toe caught on a bubblegum root. She threw herself at the protection wall, grabbing the gleaming gumdrop shard that she'd knocked out of place. Her fingernails scrabbled against the soft caramel skin of the apple, digging out the sugary glue. She stuck it into the crack, hoping it'd be enough.

The glint of the wolf-claw sword shone in the corner of her eye just as she slammed the gumdrop slab back into place.

The magic was instant. Not the small tingle she'd felt earlier, like a glimpse of sunlight. This was a torrent. A jet of water that crashed across the cottage and garden and sent the intruders flying.

They smashed into the icy ground at the edge of the forest in a tangle of limbs and silver. With the spell back in place, they wouldn't be able to see the cottage even if they stumbled into it.

Maud sat back on her heels and let out a low sigh of relief. They were safe.

Not only that, but she'd done it. She'd fixed a spell all by herself.

A sound made her turn around. Grim was scratching at the door with a low whine.

She smiled at him. "All right, I'm sure I can sneak you some shortbread before Agatha comes back."

She pushed open the door, letting Grim nudge through first. Then she froze.

A fire burned in the oven, so hot it seared her all the way from the doorway. The table had been knocked over, the cauldron spilling its contents onto the floor.

But that wasn't what had made Maud stop. What made her freeze was the sight of the animals creeping out from hiding places, their faces stricken. Nuss peeked her nose out from behind a sugar pot, her tail quivering.

Maud's mouth was dry when she spoke, "Where's Mother Agatha?"

Florian hopped toward her. "The Wolves." He looked up at her, his hooded eyes sad. "They pushed her in the fire."

4

A WITCH'S ASHES

"But I sent the Wolves away," Maud whispered. "We were meant to be safe."

The whole world seemed to tilt. The solid ground she'd always stood on roiling beneath her feet. Agatha had always been there. Sometimes disapproving, sometimes infuriating. But always *there*.

Tears stung Maud's eyes, hot as dragon spice. How had this happened?

Nuss hopped over to her, nuzzling her soft nose against her hand. The squirrel let out a low sniffle.

The sound broke something in Maud's chest, as if her

gingerbread center had cracked. A sharp fracture in her heart that couldn't be fixed like a crumbled cake.

Maud shook her head, tears slipping down her face. "She's not gone. She can't be gone."

If Agatha was really *gone*, it was Maud's fault. She was the one who'd broken the protection spell. The one who'd ruined everything.

Her stomach churned. That wasn't all. Without Agatha to tether her creations, they'd all crumble away. Go back to being nothing but unmoving gingerbread as Agatha's magic faded.

Not just Maud, but all of them—Nuss, Florian, the little sugar mice—would be gone too. They may as well all be ashes already.

Ashes. That word caught in her mind.

She looked up. A small sliver of hope pierced through her grief. "A witch isn't truly gone until her ashes are drowned. Isn't that right?"

Florian nodded hesitantly. "Yes, I suppose. But it would take strong magic to bring her back. Strong magic that we don't have."

Maud jumped to her feet. A burning determination settled in her heart. She wouldn't give up that easily. She couldn't give up on Agatha. On any of them. "But maybe we can find someone who does."

She hurried over to the shelves and grabbed a small pink jar. She turned back to the animals. "Breadcrumbs."

Nuss hopped forward. Her ears were still pressed back nervously. "Can you get them to work?"

Maud shrugged, trying to sound more confident than she felt. "Of course."

She sat on the floor and opened the jar, staring down at the sprinkled white crumbs. Breadcrumbs were a witch's best way of tracking. They could be used to find anything, from stray ribbons to a lost dragon to a tree that blossomed only on a new moon.

And Maud could use it to find a witch near them. The Witching Guild required witches to help another witch in need. Hopefully, she'd count as enough of a witch to warrant that help. She had to.

Maud desperately wanted to find someone else who knew what to do. She wanted an adult to tell her it would all be okay. That would normally be Agatha. Or sometimes Florian—but even he looked as lost as Maud felt.

She blinked down at the jar of breadcrumbs. She just needed to get them to work. She'd seen Agatha do it before, when she'd misplaced the whisk or needed to track down where Grim had wandered off to. The memory was painful, Agatha smiling as she sprinkled the crumbs onto the path. *We always have a way of getting home*, she'd said.

Maud hoped these breadcrumbs would be enough to save her home now.

She opened the front door and stepped out onto the patchwork macaron path. She reached for a fistful of crumbs and held them up. She glanced back at the others, all watching her with wide eyes. "Is there a spell?"

Florian shook his head. "They were enchanted when Agatha made them. Now all you have to do is concentrate."

Concentrate sounded a lot easier than it actually was. Maud found it rather difficult to concentrate when her heart was hammering and everything was falling apart around her.

She closed her eyes and tightened her fist around the crumbs. She tried to remember that small spark of magic she'd felt from the cauldron. The rolling power of the protection spell. But the breadcrumbs didn't feel quite like that.

It was more like a tiny flutter. Delicate butterfly wings against her ribcage.

She'd never actually met another witch, so she didn't know quite what to picture. She tried to think of that distinct aura of magic that always sizzled around Agatha. That would have to be enough.

The fluttering got stronger. It whispered around Maud's chest like a spider's web, then burst out. Maud inhaled sharply and dropped the breadcrumbs.

She opened her eyes. The crumbs had formed a line on the path, glittering as if dusted with sugar crystals. Despite everything, she felt a grin spread across her face. She'd done it. All she had to do now was follow the trail.

She hurried back inside the cottage. There was no way of knowing how far she'd have to travel to find another witch. She'd need supplies. So she grabbed one of the linen packs Agatha used when she went in search of new ingredients.

Maud picked up some bread from the gleaming peppermint sideboard. Her stomach twisted as she remembered Agatha bringing the loaf out of the oven, the spices sifting through the air. Maud's eyes stung, but she blinked the tears away as she stowed the loaf in her pack. She added some dried fruit, a parcel of cookies, another spiced loaf, and a small bag of food for Grim.

A fresh batch of Agatha's heart-shaped gingerbread charms still sat on a baking tray, as if waiting for her to come back. Agatha saved those treats for hard days, pulling them out of the little purple jar when she needed to make Maud smile. Mother Agatha always said gingerbread was the most important part of magic, the true heart of any great spell.

Maud knew they weren't practical (she obviously couldn't *eat* gingerbread) and there wasn't really room for them, but she slipped one of the little hearts into her pocket anyway. It felt like bringing a bit of Agatha's warmth with her, a comforting hug in the midst of all this.

Nuss hopped over to her. She held out Agatha's leather travel roll, filled with emergency ingredients in tinkling glass vials. Maud took it gratefully. She was glad Nuss was on board with this plan. It made it feel more possible.

Florian fluttered down onto the counter, one talon on Agatha's great spellbook. "We should take this."

"You're coming?" Maud asked, surprised and deeply relieved.

"Obviously," Florian replied. "You could hardly manage this without me."

A little more of the fear eased in Maud's chest. Even

with his condescending help, she was pleased to have the vulture. Maybe his lectures would even come in handy.

She took the spellbook from Florian's talon. It was heavy and perhaps cumbersome, but they couldn't leave it. The book and the ingredients made her feel more prepared. More like a real witch than a little gingerbread girl who was in over her head.

Maud glanced at the oven, its flames finally dying. She'd have to collect the ashes and keep them safe. Even the slightest bit of water could stop Agatha from being able to come back properly. She picked up one of the fresh ingredient jars Agatha kept on hand, made from sugar spun with unicorn horn. She liked to claim it was the strongest substance ever made.

Maud hoped it would be strong enough to keep Agatha's ashes safe.

5
FOLLOW THE BREADCRUMBS

Maud followed the glimmering trail of breadcrumbs into the line of trees. They lay spread across the forest floor like a carpet of stars, as if the sky and ground had been inverted. Florian scouted ahead to make sure the Wolves weren't still on the prowl, while Nuss sat on Maud's shoulder, shelling hazelnuts. Grim snuffled up the scraps as she dropped them, which definitely couldn't be good for him, but Maud would deal with that later.

Every few paces, her fingers drifted up to the glass vial of ashes hung on a leather cord around her neck, both to check they were safe and to try to draw some comfort from Agatha's presence. But no matter how many times she clenched the tiny jar, Maud still felt like a very small girl wandering alone in a vast wood.

There was no telling how long it would take to find a witch. Their cottage was remote as it was, and witches tended to travel alone. A powerful witch could step through a sunbeam and appear half a continent away in less time than it took Maud to blink. It could be an impossible task.

But she'd have to do it. No matter how long it took.

Except it *did* matter how long it took, Maud remembered with a painful twinge. She didn't have all the time in the world to search for a witch, not now. She only had until Agatha's magic faded. Maud looked down at her hands, already imagining them crumbling back to gingerbread.

A low whistle from up ahead made her pause. She squinted into the green shadows to make out Florian's fluttering wings. He landed inelegantly on the ground, panting hard. His feathers stood out on his neck, his soft honey eyes wide.

"Wolves."

Maud heard them then—too late. Two figures crested the scraggy knoll in front of her, their masks leering.

Abandoning the trail of crumbs, Maud dove into the tangled brush.

How had the Wolves found her so quickly?

Unless they'd never left. Just hung around in the woods, hoping to smoke out another witch… And she'd walked right into their trap.

Their shouts echoed after her as she pounded through the trees, branches whipping against her face and tearing at her clothes. They wouldn't be able to follow her through the dense undergrowth, not with their heavy swords and long cloaks. If she could just get far enough away, she'd be safe.

"Watch out!" Nuss squeaked, as a stray branch nearly dislodged her from Maud's shoulder. The squirrel grabbed fistfuls of Maud's hair to stop from toppling off. "There's another branch— Careful, my hair bow!"

The marzipan bow caught on the tangle of thorns and fell to the muddy ground.

Nuss tugged on Maud's hair. "I said be careful. We need to go back for it!"

"Your bow isn't my first priority when running for our

lives," Maud panted, ducking under a twisted trunk covered in emerald green moss. "Anyway, it'll grow back."

Or, at least, Maud hoped it would. Would that change without Agatha?

Nuss let out a little *hmph* of annoyance.

Maud risked a glance back over her shoulder. It was full dark now, only the smallest trickle of moonlight through the branches. But she knew this wood well, even at night. It lay still around her. No sound of Wolves prowling toward her, of drawn swords or snarling yells.

She let out a ragged breath and slowed down. They hadn't managed to follow through the dense brush.

Grim bounded up to her, twigs snared in his violet fur. She scratched his ears as Florian landed on the branch above her head.

"I think they turned back," the vulture croaked.

Nuss risked peeking out from Maud's tangled hair. She frowned up at Florian. "Are you sure?"

Florian ruffled his feathers irritably. "Certainly. A vulture prides itself on the finest eyesight of any bird—"

"I thought that was eagles?"

"Eagles!?" Florian squawked. "I will have you know that propaganda—"

"Let's get back to the breadcrumbs," Maud cut in before they could argue anymore. Once Florian got started on eagles, there was no stopping him.

She had enough crumbs left that if they could find a clear path, she'd be able to get back on the trail.

She pushed through a tangle of willow leaves, and Grim let out a low rumble—his attempt at a growl. She'd opened her mouth to ask why when she saw for herself. The ground seemed to drop out from under her.

The two Wolves stood ahead of her in a neat clearing, not more than ten paces away. They must have cut around, guessing where she was going.

The nearest one turned at the sound. Hollow, masked eyes fixed on Maud. "There's the little witchling." His voice was a deep rumble in the quiet.

This close, she realized that these weren't the same Wolves who'd been in the cottage. This pair was much taller, broad shouldered and towering over her. One held a sword almost as tall as Maud, while the other brandished a wicked-looking dagger with a shining quartz handle.

There was no hint of humor in their gravelly voices, only a cold certainty. Wolves that had found their prey.

A whole pack of them, in her woods—how had that

happened? How could they have gone from something that wasn't meant to be real to this?

She turned to run, but her sleeve caught on the dangling willow branches. The two Wolves lunged forward, swords ready. Nuss threw one of her hazelnuts, but the Wolf just batted it away. Florian flew at the other, smothering their face in a whirl of frosting.

Maud tore at her sleeve, the snagging branches holding tight. But just as it wrenched free, a firm hand grabbed her.

She tried to pull away, but the grip was like iron. The other Wolf finally threw Florian off in a flutter of sugar feathers and turned their attention to Maud as well. Two snarling masks bearing down on her.

Her fingers scrambled at her belt, searching it for something that could help her. With her mind racing, she couldn't remember what she'd put in there. Agatha had never told her what to do in this situation—this sort of situation should never have happened. Maud's eyes stung. More than anything, she wished Agatha were here. Wished she could appear in a shower of flour and make the Wolves flee with their tails between their legs.

But Agatha wasn't here. It was up to Maud.

She picked a vial at random, praying to the First Witch that it was something useful, and threw it at the man's face.

It hit the snout of his mask, leaving a splintered dent as it burst open. Reddish-orange powder flew everywhere—cinnamon, from the smell of it. But it wasn't accompanied by any flash of magic, no stirring in Maud's gut. It was just a spice.

But even a spice will hurt if it gets in your eyes.

Maud had learned that the hard way the first time she rolled cinnamon twists, and the two Wolves were about to realize the same thing.

The Wolf released her and stumbled back, scrabbling at his mask, while the other let out an anguished hiss.

Maud grabbed Nuss—ignoring the squirrel's complaints—and broke into a run. Florian swooped after her, followed by Grim's bounding paws.

Maud had no idea where she was going—where she *could* go that the Wolves wouldn't follow. She had no magic to use, no places to hide. All she could do was keep putting one foot in front of the other.

Angry yells followed her, echoing against the trees, so at least one of the Wolves had recovered from the ingredient attack.

"They're getting closer!" Nuss squeaked, covering her eyes.

Maud's legs burned already with the effort. She couldn't go any faster. Especially not slipping and sliding over the loose twigs and muddy ground. Maybe if they could just make it to the edge of the woods, they'd find somewhere better to hide.

Her foot caught on a stray tree root, and she went tumbling forward with a crash. The last of the breadcrumbs flew from her hand. Her only chance at finding help gone.

But as she lay there trying to catch her breath, fingers pressing into the dirt, something lit up ahead of her.

The fallen breadcrumbs had illuminated, far brighter than before.

Maud didn't have any other hope, so she scrabbled after the new trail. It wound around a large hollow trunk, though she could see no sign of any witch. The wooded trees ahead looked as empty as before.

And then, quite suddenly—in the space between one footfall and the next—she wasn't in the woods at all.

6
THE BEWITCHING HOLLOW

Maud skittered to a halt. The shouts and hurried footsteps vanished. The crisp smell of leaves and damp scent of mud had disappeared too, replaced with something slightly too sweet—like caramel just about to turn.

She stood in what she could only describe as a tree trunk, though it was far bigger than any tree she'd ever seen. The space was twice as wide as Agatha's cottage and at least three times as tall, lined with moss in all different shades, everything from the bright orange of sunset to the pale violet of Grim's hair. It was spun into all sorts of shapes: Normal things like chairs and a table, but stranger objects sat among them. A coral-pink chess set with pieces shaped like body parts. A moss chandelier that hung, unsuspended, with gleaming green flames. And in one corner, a massive moss cauldron of darkest indigo.

Maud turned in a slow circle, trying to take it all in. She'd seen strange, unexplainable things all her life, but this was undoubtedly the strangest. She'd grown up in a house made of gingerbread, but the magic that buzzed in the air here had none of the cottage's comfort.

"Where are we?" she asked the creatures in a low whisper, anticipating a lecture from Florian.

"This is a Bewitching Hollow."

Maud whirled around. A figure stood by the cauldron—one Maud was sure hadn't been there a moment ago.

"A...Bewitching Hollow?" Maud repeated. She'd never heard of anything like that before.

The woman took a step forward.

The light cast by the odd moss-candles illuminated her face. Sharp cheekbones, neat blonde hair and emerald-painted lips. She wore a dark green cloak with a glinting emblem pinned to the collar: *W* and *G* intertwined with twisting vines.

Maud had never seen the symbol in person before, but she knew it well enough.

"The Witching Guild," Florian croaked, awed into surprising silence.

Relief flooded through Maud. "I—I've been looking for you."

The woman tilted her head. Her eyes—the same green as her cloak—caught the light like a cat's. "Looking for me?"

"Yes," Maud said quickly. "I mean, not *you* you. But a witch."

The witch raised her eyebrows in question. "Why do you need a witch?"

Now that Maud was standing in front of someone who could help her, she suddenly didn't know what to say. How did she explain everything that had happened? Even Nuss was speechless for once—though that might have been because she was more preoccupied with grooming the stray twigs out of her fur. The squirrel always had very particular priorities.

"I—" Maud swallowed and pushed on. "I'm Mother Agatha's apprentice."

"Oh, you're Agatha's little witchling," the witch said at once. "Did she have a message for me?"

Maud blinked. She hadn't expected the witch to know Agatha. But she supposed it made sense that Agatha had acquaintances Maud didn't know. After all, Maud was the one who'd been restricted to the cottage and nearby woods, not Agatha.

Maud opened her mouth to try to speak and found she couldn't. Instead, a sob shook through her chest.

The woman hurried forward, bending down to Maud's eye level and putting gentle hands on her shoulders. "Oh, my dear, what is it?"

Fresh tears spilled from Maud's eyes, and the whole terrible story came pouring out. The spell that went wrong, the argument. The unexpected visitor and Maud's mistake— she faltered here, afraid the witch would reprimand her, but the woman just nodded at her to keep going. So Maud told her about the ashes. About all of Agatha's creations and what would happen to them, then finally about the Wolves in the wood and how she'd appeared in here.

When Maud was finished, the woman ushered her into a surprisingly comfortable moss chair and set about making tea.

Maud hiccupped as she accepted a steaming mug—also made, predictably, of moss. Now that her tears had run out, a prickle of embarrassment wormed its way in. What would such a powerful witch think of her?

"Thank you," she mumbled, pressing her hands around the warm cup. It was slightly squishy to the touch. Grim nudged his nose against her hand, but she shook him off. After all the hazelnut shells he'd eaten, she certainly wasn't going to give him unidentifiable moss tea.

The witch pulled up a chair next to her, holding a steaming mug of her own. "My name's Vira," she said.

"I'm Maud."

Staring down into the purplish liquid, Maud tried to work up to asking the question she was scared to voice. Instead, she blurted, "What is this place?"

"Like I said, it's a Bewitching Hollow," Vira replied. "A safe haven for witches. If you're in trouble or need somewhere to sleep or hide from a storm, you'll always find one."

Maud blinked. Agatha had never mentioned them to her. Though, since Maud wasn't meant to stray far from the cottage, it had never really mattered. She glanced over at Florian, who was perched on the mossy table, but he looked just as uncertain as she felt.

"Agatha never showed you one?" Vira asked, her face creased with concern.

Maud shook her head, her cheeks burning. She took a sip of the tea to distract from the moment and was pleasantly surprised to find it didn't taste of moss. It was a mix of sweet, dark plum and some kind of spice. Maybe cardamom.

It gave her the courage to ask the question she'd been dreading. She took a shaking breath. "Can you help her?"

The witch sat forward, her emerald lips turned down in worry. "I can't," she said. The two words fell heavy in the room. They sank into Maud's stomach like stones.

She clutched the cup, her knuckles white. "But you have to. I can't— I don't—"

Vira held up a hand. "I can't help," she said again. "But I think you can."

Florian's yellow eyes widened, and Nuss let out a squeak, pausing in the preening of her newly regrown marzipan bow.

Maud stared up at the witch, sure she'd misheard. "Me?"

Vira nodded. "Only the First Witch could resurrect witches from their ashes. Her spellbook would hold the answers, but it's buried in an ancient glade, long since lost."

58

"So how can we find it?" Maud asked.

"*We* can't. The glade is enchanted so that no creature of flesh and blood can enter, yet the spellbook can only be touched by a witch."

"Then, it's hopeless."

"Perhaps not." Vira's green eyes cut into Maud, all too knowing. "Because you are not quite *flesh and blood*, are you?"

Maud's heart stuttered. "How do you—"

Vira gave a small smile. "I've been around enough of Agatha's spells to recognize them."

Maud shifted in her seat. She didn't like the idea of someone knowing what she was just by looking. She spent all her time trying to prove her human-ness, and this woman only had to glance at her to know she was a fake.

She looked up at Vira. "But how would I find the spellbook? It could be anywhere."

Vira's face shifted into a smile—a smile that was all together not encouraging. "The Witching Guild has been searching for that answer for centuries. But I think I may have a clue."

She reached over to her leather pack and pulled out a cracked scroll. She spread it on her lap, smoothing the curled edges. Maud leaned over to stare at the squiggly lines. Some of them she recognized—the green mass of the wood she'd been in, the reflective lake where Agatha traded for mermaid scales. But most of it was new, a vast and unknown land.

"I've been tracking a fairy-tale book," Vira explained, running her finger over the map. "One that is said to contain the first tales of witches." She pointed to the small diamond just beyond the woods that marked the Dragon's Library. "I finally found it here. Though the old dragon wasn't willing to part with it, I did manage to get a peek. And it showed me what I believe to be the location of the First Witch's spellbook."

"Where?"

"In the Abandoned Forest."

"That's in the Shadelands," Florian said. "Impossible. That's far too dangerous."

Maud gasped. For once, she agreed with Florian. She couldn't go there, human or not. It was a place of eternal darkness, where all sorts of long-forgotten monsters roamed.

"The perfect hiding place," Vira said, her eyes alight. "The spellbook is said to be hidden in the darkest part of a gladed forest, a place so powerful that not even sunlight dares enter. Dangerous, perhaps. But certainly not impossible."

Maud shook her head. "I can't go there."

Vira's mouth pressed into a sad line—the way Agatha's did when she had to tell Maud her biscuits had burned. "I'm afraid that's the only way to bring her back."

"You can't risk it," Florian croaked. He hopped forward, nuzzling his chocolate beak against her arm. "It would be perilous for even the most seasoned witch. You're only a fledgling."

Maud glanced up at Vira, biting her lip. "How long until Mother Agatha's magic fades from…us?"

"I can't say. Perhaps days, perhaps weeks. Certainly no more than a cycle of the moon."

Maud gritted her teeth. She looked between Florian and Nuss, two of Agatha's most beautiful creations, both bursting with so much life she couldn't bear to imagine them gone. She looked down at her own hands, which would crumble to gingerbread as Agatha's magic faded, and over at Grim who would be left all alone.

Maud wouldn't let that happen. No matter the risk, she wouldn't let all of Agatha's magic be destroyed by Maud's mistake. She might be a fledgling, but that didn't mean she couldn't do this.

She had to. For Agatha. For all of them.

Maud didn't look at Florian as she spoke, her voice determined. "I'll do it."

7
GONE
TRAVELING

It took less time than Maud would have expected to pre-pare to go to the Shadelands. She wasn't sure if that was a sign of how few supplies there were in the Bewitching Hollow or because no amount of equipment would pre-pare her for the horrors of the Abandoned Forest.

Florian had insisted they rest first before heading out. "After all," he'd said, "there's no use going off on a ridicu-lous quest on tired wings."

Nuss and Maud had both complained—Maud about the time pressure and the squirrel about her dislike of staying still—but Maud couldn't deny she did feel a little better after some sleep.

In the end, Maud set off with some moss cakes (according to Vira, they were very *nutritious*, but Maud wasn't sure they were worth the smell), a map, and somewhat vague instructions on how to reach the town of Gone, the last safe place before the Shadelands.

All Vira had done was wave Maud in the direction of a purple, sprouting mushroom and told her to *follow the Toadstool Path*. Maud was beginning to wonder if part of witch training involved learning how to speak only in confusing riddles.

Maud turned to say as much to Vira, but the witch had vanished into thin air.

Well, when Maud was a full-fledged witch she'd make sure to give detailed instructions. None of this ambiguous nonsense followed by disappearing mysteriously.

If, whispered a voice in her head. *If* she ever became a full-fledged witch. Without Agatha, Maud wouldn't reach her next birthday, let alone finish her training.

Maud glared down at the purple mushroom, deciding to direct her annoyance at it instead. It didn't form anything vaguely resembling a path. Just a lone mushroom clinging to a hollow trunk. And it was definitely a mushroom, not a toadstool. Well, she was pretty sure. She'd never really understood the difference.

"What am I supposed to do now?" she asked the empty forest.

Florian ruffled his wings from his nearby perch. "You follow the Toadstool Path, of course."

Maud was very tempted to throw the mushroom at him.

He seemed to sense her annoyance, adding, "Picture the place you want to go and look for the next toadstool."

Maud let out a huff. That wasn't much more helpful. She couldn't see any other mushrooms—or toadstools—and how was she supposed to picture her destination? She'd never been to Gone before. How did you even go to a place called Gone?

Great. Now she was thinking in riddles.

"Look!" Nuss called, pointing into the distant trees. "Over there!"

Maud squinted into the gloom. Sure enough, the faint outline of a poisonous green mushroom glowed against a crop of brambles.

She was pretty sure it hadn't been there before, but

Maud was used to things appearing and disappearing without explanation.

She hurried over to it, Grim trotting alongside her while Florian flew overhead and Nuss clutched on to Maud's hair.

For a minute, she couldn't see any other mushrooms beyond the bright green one and was certain this must've just been a coincidence. But then she spotted another, a little farther away this time. This one was butter yellow with orange splotches. It seemed friendlier than the first. But the next one was a dusty pink that reminded her painfully of home. She hurried on from that one.

With each mushroom, the landscape around her changed. Subtly at first, the trees shifting in color and the flowers swaying in a new wind. The snow melted away with a bright red mushroom, and light broke through the trees at the sight of an inky-black cap.

"Why's it called the Toadstool Path when we're following mushrooms?" Maud asked.

Florian looked aghast. "Do you mean to tell me you still do not know the difference between mushrooms and toadstools?" He began a long and very tedious lecture, detailing the minute differences, which made Maud regret she'd said anything at all.

And she was still convinced they were mushrooms.

Finally, as they reached a mushroom as blue as the summer sky, the forest faded away. It was replaced with a dusty road and a large wooden gate set into a stone wall so tall she couldn't see the top. Painted above the gate, in licorice-black lettering, was one word: Gone.

The town of Gone was unlike any place Maud had ever been. Granted, she hadn't really been anywhere that wasn't Agatha's cottage or the surrounding forest. But still, Gone was unlike any place she'd ever imagined.

There were people everywhere. Probably more people than Maud had seen in her entire lifetime. Shopkeepers and travelers milled about, unpacking boxes and selling any number of strange and impractical things like little figurines that didn't move and mint tea. Who'd ever heard of tea without frog scales in it?

Among the humans, she spotted a few imps hauling precious stones, along with the shimmering green of goblins and little shoe-elves. They mingled easily with the humans, their chattering tones all mixing together.

Maud didn't think she saw any witches, though. Not that

witches were always easy to spot from their appearances, but she didn't feel the distinct sizzle of magic.

There were creatures too. Some in tiny cages, all squeaking like sugar mice. Some lurking around their owners' feet, like Grim. Some massive beasts with glowing pink horns that pulled huge wagons. Squawking embercrows with their scorched feathers, and fanged night demons with empty eye sockets. All touched with magic but not *made* from it like Maud, Nuss, and the others.

It made Maud suddenly feel very separate. A fraud who'd be spotted at any moment.

On the horizon, just where the town petered out to nothing, was a dark expanse. Like a distant gathering storm. The Shadelands.

It was all too much. Unfamiliar sights and sounds bursting in her brain like overboiled custard. The animals didn't like it either. Nuss hid in Maud's hood, and Grim stayed so close to her ankles she almost tripped over him.

Maud saw an empty alleyway to her right and dove for it. She took a deep breath, relishing the brief quiet.

"I'm beginning to see why witches like staying in cottages," she murmured. "It's too hectic out here."

Florian swept down from where he'd been flying above,

getting a vulture's-eye view of the town. "That's not why witches live in cottages," he said, clearly eager for the chance of another lecture. "They live in isolated and protected places so they don't get bothered by humans looking for spells."

"Or children trying to steal pieces of their house," Nuss added.

"And traditionally, of course," Florian went on, unperturbed, "the isolation offered protection from Wolves. An interesting feature of—"

"Do we need to worry about Wolves here?" Maud asked, cutting the lecture short. It seemed like all sorts of people came through Gone, and even if they weren't actively calling for witches to be burned, there could still be enemies among them.

"No," Florian replied with a ruffle of wings. "Wolves are mostly extinct now. Everyone knows that."

Maud shot him a look. "*Mostly* being the operative word."

She looked back at the shadows on the horizon. "So I suppose we just walk toward the big, dark, scary place?"

Florian shook his head. "You cannot simply *walk in*. Do you want to get eaten by a crested nesslebusser?" he asked with a tone of supreme superiority. "Or torn apart by night ravens?"

"I wouldn't mind you getting torn apart," Maud muttered, earning her a snort from Nuss.

Florian's sharp eyes narrowed. "What was that?"

"Nothing, your cleverness. So, what should I do?"

Florian ruffled his feathers, pleased to have all the answers. "You'll have to join a convoy, of course."

A convoy, as Florian patronizingly explained, was a group of travelers who entered the Shadelands together for protection, either to transport goods or seek out rare fruits or just to explore the darkness. Maud wasn't sure she could trust anyone foolish enough to venture in there willingly, but she had to admit their options were limited.

At the very edge of the strange town sat a wide square. Well, more of a hexagon, really, but the sign claimed it was The Last Square. Lots of windy roads and paths led into it, but only one led out. Stone paved and wide enough for Agatha's entire cottage—if it chose to sprout legs and go for a walk—the road wound its way toward the distant clouds of the Shadelands.

Just like the rest of Gone, the square was a mess of

people. If entering the town had been overwhelming, this was ten times worse. Carts and packages and more strange creatures Maud couldn't name, all pressing in around them.

But Maud focused on what they needed. She aimed for a booth on one side of the hexagon marked with a gleaming gold compass. It took a fair amount of jostling and ducking to avoid flying parcels and elbows, but Maud finally reached it. Florian fluttered down to perch on the top point of the compass. He stared down at them with the air of someone who was bored of waiting.

Show-off, Maud thought. It was much easier to navigate this town with wings.

The counter was so high Maud had to stretch onto her tiptoes to see over it. There was no one there, just a small sign that unhelpfully read Gone Traveling.

"Is that the name?" Maud muttered to Nuss. "Or does that mean they're off traveling?"

Nuss shrugged, scrabbling from Maud's shoulder onto the wooden countertop. "I think there's someone back there." She banged a small paw on the counter. "Hello? *Hello?*"

A red-faced man with bushier eyebrows than Florian

appeared. "Well," he exclaimed, looking down at Nuss with greedy interest. "How unusual."

Nuss leaped back onto Maud's shoulder, sending flecks of hazelnut mousse flying.

The man leaned over the counter, looking down at Maud. "What is that thing?"

Nuss let out a huff of annoyance as she hid behind Maud's hair. "Not a *thing*. A squirrel."

His bushy eyebrows flew into his hair. "It speaks?"

Maud got the sudden, uncomfortable feeling that perhaps it wasn't normal for most people in the town of Gone to come across a talking squirrel made out of cake. Of course she'd seen fur squirrels in the forest, with their nut-brown fluff instead of buttercream and their tiny chirrups. She'd seen birds with feathers instead of meringue.

But until this very moment she hadn't realized that meant Florian, Nuss, and all the others were so unusual.

What would these people think of Maud if they knew she was made from gingerbread too?

She cleared her throat to try to cover Nuss's harrumph-ing. "I want to join a convoy," Maud said, glad she sounded more confident than she felt, "into the Shadelands."

The man's expression went from curious to amused. "What's a little girl like you looking for in the Shadelands?"

"Uhh—" Something made Maud shy away from the truth. Searching for the spellbook of the First Witch to help resurrect her mother didn't seem like something she should announce in front of this man. "I'm looking for unusual fruit," she improvised, "for my mother's bakery."

The man didn't look convinced. "And do you have gold to pay for that?"

Maud bit her lip. She hadn't thought of that either. They never usually used money, just traded for whatever supplies or ingredients they needed.

"I have cookies," she said, pulling out one of her little parcels. Agatha had always said her cookies were worth their weight in gold. "Peppermint and chocolate," Maud added.

The man did not take the cookies.

"We only accept gold," he said. "But…" His eyes drifted toward Nuss's rather ineffective hiding place in Maud's short hair. "I'm sure we could work out a trade."

Maud took a sharp step back. She didn't like the sound of that.

"That strange squirrel would be payment enough."

"Certainly not!" Nuss said indignantly.

That seemed to be the wrong thing to say, as all it did was send his eyes wide as saucers again. Before Maud could speak, the man lunged across the counter.

Nuss dug her scrabbly claws into Maud's shoulder. "Run!"

Maud didn't need to be told twice. She didn't even need to be told once, her feet already moving as she dove back into the crowd. She ducked through tangled legs and weaved around crates, Grim close behind her. The man's shouts chased after them, but he couldn't dodge people so easily. For once, her height (or lack thereof) was an advantage.

She threw herself under a cart and rolled out the other side—right into a dead end. Piles of crates and bundles of medicinal herbs blocked her path. The owner was too busy fussing over his tall moon-elk to notice them.

The man's shouts and pounding footsteps still followed them. Too close.

"Quick," she whispered to Grim. She pushed him behind one of the bundles of herbs into a large crate.

She followed and pulled the lid closed behind her. Feeling her way in the dark, she crawled past supplies and firewood—this really was a *huge* crate—until she reached the far end. Even if the man saw the crate, there was no way he'd think to look all the way back here.

She couldn't see where Florian had gone but trusted that he had the good sense to hide on one of the nearby rooftops.

The angry yells seemed to be getting farther away now, but Maud didn't want to risk going back out into the open yet.

She held Grim close on one side, and Nuss snuggled against her neck on the other. Maud was beginning to understand why Agatha didn't like going out into the world. The cottage was much nicer.

Maud would give anything to be back in the warmth of the cottage. Agatha would be boiling up some cinnamon toffee for teatime, Maud dusting a Bundt cake in lemon sugar in the corner. Everyone safe and together. She blinked, and a few tears escaped.

"Um," Nuss said, distracting Maud from her sadness. "Why is the floor moving?"

Maud's heart lurched. Nuss was right, the floor *was* moving. Or, more accurately, the crate was moving. With a juddering bump, it was thrown onto a rapidly moving cart.

Maud peered through one of the narrow gaps in the wood to see Gone *going* behind her. They were on the wide road toward the Shadelands.

Well, it wasn't quite as they'd planned, but at least they'd made it to some sort of convoy. She hoped Florian would manage to follow them.

As the cart bumped around a turn, a flash of sunlight burst through the slats. It lit up the stacked objects around her. Where a moment before, her heart had jumped, it now felt as if it might've stopped all together.

It turned out Florian had been wrong for once.

Too bad Maud would probably never get a chance to say "I told you so."

Because it wasn't just supplies that she was crouched behind. It was weapons. Weapons adorned with claws and snarling fangs.

Wolves.

Common
Spells for
Uncommon
Witchery

8
A WITCH AMONG THE WOLVES

Maud felt the moment they entered the Shadelands. Even without the thick darkness that clenched around them, swallowing the faintest glimmer, she would have been able to feel it. Like the press of a rough blanket against her skin. A low buzzing of distant magic.

She shivered, pulling Grim's warmth closer. Now all she could see when she peered through the slats was the soft ring of light cast by the moon-elk. She guessed that was why they brought the strange, translucent creatures. It was easier than wasting torches.

Maud had read stories about that. Even fires were swallowed by the darkness of the Shadelands.

She tried to read the map, to form some kind of plan, but none of the moon-elks' light reached inside the cart. Even if she could read it, she wasn't sure how she'd know if they were headed toward the Abandoned Forest. Were there signposts in the Shadelands?

Just as she was considering that—and realizing her legs were beginning to cramp from being curled up so tight—a very worrying thing happened: Nuss got bored.

It was a well-known occurrence in the cottage, one they were always on the lookout for. Because when Nuss got bored, destruction usually followed.

It began slowly, with the squirrel fidgeting in Maud's hood. Then she started humming—ignoring all Maud's attempts to shush her—and poking her head out. Before Maud could stop her, Nuss hopped down to start exploring the contents of the crate.

Maud tried to grab her but was rewarded with mousse on her fingertips and an impossible squirrel climbing into the far reaches of the crate.

"Why do you think they need so many weapons?" Nuss asked, much louder than Maud would've liked.

"Probably to skewer you when they hear you," Maud hissed back.

But Nuss ignored her. She sniffed one of the bundles. *"Eugh,"* she proclaimed. "They have such bad taste in perfume."

Something told Maud that wasn't perfume, but it didn't seem like the moment to bring it up.

Florian would've been useful right about now. Not that Maud would ever tell him, but he had a way of calming Nuss down and making her listen. Unlike Maud, who may as well have been silent for all the squirrel was listening to her.

Where was he now? Maud wondered with an anxious jolt. He might not have seen them get in the crates. He could still be stuck in Gone, wondering where they had run off to.

Nuss kept climbing, following her snuffling nose higher and higher up the piles of objects. Piles of *precarious* objects.

"Nuss, you're going to knock something—"

Crash!

One of the swords tipped against the next, a domino reaction of clattering metal.

Maud held her breath. Maybe they hadn't heard. Maybe—

The cart jerked to a halt. Muffled voices called out to each other, then soft footsteps. She pulled back into the darkest shadows, shoving Nuss underneath a bundle of herbs and tucking Grim behind her.

The back of the cart swung open, and a soft light, similar to the glow of the moon-elk, swung across the space. The woman holding it was tall with graying hair and gruff features that reminded Maud of rye rolls.

If this woman were one of Agatha's creations, she'd definitely be made of that dense, seeded bread. The kind of bread that survived somewhere like the Shadelands.

Maud couldn't see one of those wolf-headed swords strapped to the woman's side, but she still didn't like her chances. She reached for her belt, popping the cork out of the vial of cardamom. Not quite as strong as cinnamon, but still nasty if it got in your eyes.

The light swung away from her, toward the other side of the cart.

Maud relaxed a little—which turned out to be a mistake. Her already cramping limbs decided that was their

cue to relax as well. It made her hand jerk, specks of cardamom flying through the air. Right toward her nose.

It was too late—Maud couldn't stop it. She sneezed, and
a huge puff of beige powder burst around her.

The light flashed back to her. The lid flew off the crate
to reveal the woman towering over her. Icy fear spread
through Maud as she squinted in the sudden brightness.
Grim let out a low growl, more scared than intimidating.

There was nowhere to go. Maud may as well have led
them into a trap.

The woman sniffed. "Is that nutmeg?" Her voice was
stern but not angry, to Maud's relief.

"It's cardamom," Maud said automatically.

The woman tilted her head. "Huh."

Then she reached out a hand to Maud, pulling her out
of the crate and to her feet. Nuss had the good sense to
stay hidden this time.

"And what are you doing in there with your cardamom?"
the woman asked.

Maud clasped her hands behind her back, making sure
her witchmark was well out of sight. "I'm collecting rare
fruit," she said quickly, deciding it was easier to stick to
one lie, "for my mother's bakery."

But that didn't work on this woman any better than it had on the man at Gone Traveling. "By hiding in a crate at the back of a convoy?"

"Uhh," Maud stammered. "Yes, that's where you find all the rarest fruit."

"I'm sure it is."

Changing tactics, Maud grasped for something Wolves would believe. "The truth is I just…really hate witches. So I wanted to travel with the Wolves. And—and learn from them." Just saying the words made her mouth taste bitter as ground coffee.

That didn't seem to work either. The woman narrowed her eyes. "How old are you?"

Why did everyone keep asking that? Maud stuck out her chin in defiance. "Old enough."

She nodded to Grim, tucked close to Maud's ankles. "And who's your friend?"

"That's my dog," Maud said, hoping his lilac fluff wasn't visible in the near dark. "Just a dog." She shifted slightly to make sure Nuss, the very definitely not-normal squirrel, was still hidden.

The woman let out a sigh that made it sound like she was giving up. "Well, we can't turn around now anyway," she said. "We'd lose too much time, and we need to reach the Abandoned Forest before our moon-elk tire."

Before Maud had even responded, the woman began leading her back through the maze of boxes and out to the rest of the convoy. Maud shot a glance back at Nuss's hiding place, hoping the squirrel would stay quiet this time.

"My name's Rega," the woman said as she hopped down from the cart. "What's yours?"

Maud couldn't speak for a moment. She was staring at the carts spread around them, the glow of the moon-elk—and all the witch hunters looking back at her with suspicious curiosity. Weapons gleamed at their waists, and darkness spread beyond them. She glanced up at the skies, but there was no sign of Florian's familiar silhouette either.

"Your name?" Rega prompted.

Maud swallowed hard, her mouth still dry as almond flour. "Maud," she squeaked before realizing she probably shouldn't have given her real name. She wasn't exactly used to this whole undercover thing.

A young man with a burst of orange hair hurried up to them. "Is that a stowaway?"

Rega ignored him. "Maud, why don't you go sit with

the other children." She pointed to a small cart a little farther back, pulled by one of the huge moon-elk. "Make sure you stay in the cart, close to the elk's light. The kids'll show you how to make camp later."

Part of Maud wanted to run, even if there was nowhere to go but the depths of the Shadelands. That felt safer than the company of Wolves. "I could just walk…"

"I'm not risking you wandering into the Shadelands and getting snatched by a roggen," Rega replied seriously. "You know they steal children's eyes to pound into butter."

Maud bit her lip. She wasn't sure how true that was but decided she didn't want to find out. And she could hardly leave Nuss behind in that crate.

So Maud nodded and hurried over to where Rega had directed her.

She could hear Rega and the orange-haired man having some kind of argument behind her, but she barely registered it. Her heart was pounding in her ears. Today had not gone according to plan at all. Florian would be furious. As would Agatha.

But neither of them were here, so Maud just had to find some way to muddle through.

The small cart was full of Wolves only a little older than

her, though equally murderous as the grown-ups, she was sure.

She was about to climb up when she saw something that made her every muscle turn to jelly. She only just managed to cover her gasp with a cough. She recognized two of them. A girl with dark brown plaits and a sharp voice sat next to a boy with sandy hair.

She was too close now to turn and run away. But the girl barely looked up from her book, and from the way their eyes skimmed over her, they didn't remember her.

A queasy feeling tightened in her stomach. These were the people who'd been in Agatha's cottage, who'd pushed her into the fire. But if Maud let any of that slip, she'd have no way of bringing Agatha back.

Maud touched a finger to the vial of ashes hidden beneath her shirt, glad at least that Grim was at her side. He shoved his nose into her palm—even his slobbering was a comfort and enough to make her feet move. She clambered up to join the young Wolves, trying to make herself as invisible as possible. One secret witchling among a sea of witch hunters.

9
A WOLF'S FIRST HUNT

According to all the stories Agatha and Florian had told Maud, Wolves got their name from the first witch hunter family, the Wulfen. They'd been after Little Red, a powerful young witch, and decided to dress as a wolf to strike fear into her heart. They even went as far as to disguise one of them as Red's grandmother to try to trick her (which Maud really thought was excessive).

Despite all that, Little Red had outwitted them at every turn.

Maud had always liked the story, but now that she was

facing the reality, she wasn't sure she'd be up to the task like Little Red had been.

Maud kept herself tucked into the corner of the cart, trying very hard not to look at the two young Wolves she recognized. But she forgot that she needed to avoid the others' attention too. Three of them kept pointing at Grim, laughing when the wolf pup jumped at the bumping of the cart.

The one nearest her, with beady eyes and a smile like a sour lemon, spoke first. "Why's he only got three legs?"

It took precisely that one sentence for Maud to decide she didn't like any of them. Not that she was likely to, given they were Wolves. But still, it was almost impressive how easy it was to dislike them.

"Why've you only got two?" Maud shot back with a glower.

He laughed. "No need to be rude about it."

Maud was pretty sure he was the one who'd been rude, but she decided she didn't want to talk anymore.

The girl next to him leaned forward. "Are you a new apprentice?"

"Yes," Maud said, hoping that was the right answer. "I want to hunt all the witches."

"You're quite short," the girl went on with a sniff. "A witch would eat you easily."

Maud bit her tongue to stop herself from saying "Witches obviously don't eat children."

"You know," the first boy added, "Hansel's already killed a witch. He'll be one of the youngest Wolves in a century."

The sandy-haired boy—Hansel—looked vaguely embarrassed. "Not a century, Oskar," he corrected. "My dad was initiated at thirteen."

"Still," Oskar said, turning back to Maud with a glint of pride. "*One* of the youngest Wolves. When do you think you'll manage to kill a witch?"

Maud's throat stuck. Her hand clenched around the vial of ashes, everything squeezing around her.

She was saved from saying anything by an unlikely rescuer: the girl with plaits. "Do you want all of the Shadelands to hear you?" she snapped. "Because if you attract a blubeard, I won't protect you this time."

Oskar glared at her. "I don't need any protection, especially not from *you*, Gretel."

"That's not how I remember it."

The argument sufficiently distracted them from the newcomer, and Maud pulled Grim close to her. She folded herself farther into the corner. If only she could vanish into shadows or transform into a flock of ravens and fly far away. But she couldn't manage any magic close to that.

She took a shaky breath. She just had to keep her cover until the Abandoned Forest, then she'd find the spellbook and everything would be all right again. If Little Red had survived the first witch hunters, then Maud could do this.

It wasn't long before the train of wagons trundled to a stop again. Maud squinted into the darkness, trying to determine how far they'd gone. But the landscape was all the same. Empty wasteland and hollow trees as far as she could see—which wasn't very far, with only the faint glow of the moon-elk.

"Why're we stopping already?" one of the novices complained.

"You know," another replied with a pointed look at Hansel. "It's the half-moon."

The first one let out a reverent gasp.

Maud stretched—she could almost hear her limbs *pop*—and edged away from the group of children jumping down from the cart. She didn't want to know what the half-moon meant to witch hunters.

But Oskar turned his sour smile on her. "Aren't you coming, novice?" The others turned to look at her, too, all following Oskar's nosiness.

"I was just going to…" She gestured vaguely in the direction of the cargo carts. She'd hoped to avoid people and sneak away to check on Nuss, but she couldn't exactly tell them that.

"I thought you wanted to be a Wolf," Oskar said accusingly. "And you don't even want to watch Hansel's initiation?"

Maud swallowed hard. She definitely did not want to watch any kind of initiation. But if she said that, they might begin to question her story.

She put on her best even-caramel-can't-scare-me face and said, "Of course I do."

She followed the group toward the front of the convoy, where the adults were building a fire—not a normal fire, though. This one burned pale blue, similar to the strange light of the moon-elk, and hardly illuminated more than a few paces. She supposed that was the only kind of flames they could get in the Shadelands.

Maud put a reassuring hand on Grim's back. He didn't like fire very much. Sensible wolf.

The nearest adult turned toward them, and Maud almost

jumped out of her skin. They were wearing the full Wolf mask, just like Hansel and Gretel had in the cottage. Just like the grown-up Wolves who'd chased her in the woods.

But she couldn't turn and run or throw some cinnamon at them now.

It's okay, she reminded herself. *They don't know you're a witch.*

She pulled down her sleeve to make sure her witchmark was completely hidden. All the other adults—all the initiated Wolves—now had their masks on. In the strange darkness of the Shadelands, for the first time, Maud truly felt there were monsters lurking around her.

"Hansel!" One of the older Wolves came over—Maud thought it might be the orange-haired one who'd argued with Rega. "Ready?"

The other children jostled, pushing Hansel forward with cheers. Appearances or not, Maud couldn't get herself to join in with that.

"Bern, don't you think we should wait until my parents are here?" Hansel asked in a voice Maud recognized. The voice of someone clutching for excuses. But why would he want to put off his initiation? All the others seemed eager to stop being novices.

"It has to be on the half-moon, they know that." He clapped a hand on Hansel's shoulder and led him over to the periwinkle flames.

They couldn't see the moon here. No moon or stars, just endless blackness, so Maud wasn't sure how they were tracking it. The other children sat around the blaze, and Maud joined them, still holding Grim close. The rest of the convoy, in their ghoulish masks, stood on the other side of the fire, waiting.

When the flames were leaping toward the sky, so hot she wanted to scoot away from them, Bern stepped forward.

All the excited chatter stopped at once, leaving an eerie quiet.

"Tonight, we welcome Hansel to the ancient order of the Wolves," Bern called. "The last line of protection between humans and the evil witches who would steal children from their beds and eat them for breakfast."

Maud managed to cover her dismissive snort as a cough. The Wolves should really think about why they were so obsessed with cannibalism.

"The first Wolf saved this land from the tyranny of the Crimson-cloaked Witch," Bern continued. Maud frowned—was that how they told the story? "We uphold their legacy and preserve their great duty." Bern held up a small straw doll, tied with dark red ribbon. It was far from realistic, but it made Maud's insides twist.

"This is not a role to take lightly," Bern went on. Hansel stood at his side, maskless and fidgeting a little. "It is a heavy burden entrusted to us by the heroes of old. We must honor their sacrifice…"

He went on like that for a while, and Maud mostly tuned it out. *Blah-blah, witches are evil, blah-blah.* She knew the gist already. Probably a bit more child-eating in there for good measure.

As her eyes got used to the brightness of the flames, she realized not everyone around her was wearing a Wolf mask. She spotted Rega across the fire. Her face was bare, and her expression was resolutely bored. Did that mean she wasn't a Wolf? Maud had assumed everyone who traveled with them was part of the witch hunting.

It was comforting to see at least one other person not interested in the proceedings.

"And now, the witch shall burn!"

The sudden shout drew Maud back to the initiation. Hansel took the straw doll and threw it into the fire. It felt like a punch to her stomach.

She watched in horror as the doll crumbled to ashes. Her hand drifted to the vial around her neck, protective.

Hansel picked up a strange metal spoon and scooped up the doll's remains.

"And the ashes must be drowned," he finished, tipping them into a pail of water. Maud's fingers tightened. She suddenly thought she might be sick, seeing this play out in front of her. None of it was real to them. It wasn't about their mother or sister or friend.

She couldn't really duck away without it looking like she wasn't interested in joining the Wolves. People were suspicious enough already. She couldn't risk making it worse.

But she couldn't stay here, this close to the fire.

Nudging Grim with her, she shuffled back until she was a short distance from the blue firelight, near one of the supply carts. Close enough to still claim she'd been there, but far enough that she didn't feel a part of it anymore. Didn't feel like it was suffocating her.

Then she realized she was not alone.

Maud jumped. Gretel was leaning against the wooden wheel of a cart, her face hidden in the shadows. Why was Hansel's sister staying out of the celebration? Surely she should be as proud as all the other mini witch-killers.

Maud was about to try to back away before she got caught in another uncomfortable situation, when Gretel spotted her.

Maud swallowed. "I was just..."

But she was spared conjuring up a lie as Gretel spoke, scowling at the ground. "He didn't even do it, you know."

"Didn't do what?"

"Kill that witch."

Maud felt all the air rush from her lungs. It took her a moment to manage to speak, and then, her words were hoarse. "What do you mean?"

"She was already in the oven when we got there," Gretel replied. "Hansel just claimed it as his first hunt."

"But..." Maud's voice was shaky as an autumn leaf. "But why would he lie about it?"

Gretel rolled her eyes. "He just has to be the best at everything."

Maud gaped at her. Too many thoughts rushed through her brain at once. That couldn't possibly be true, could it? Maud had seen them...

No, she hadn't actually *seen* them. By the time Maud had got back, they'd just been talking about Agatha. But the creatures had said it was the Wolves...though they'd

95

been hiding. Could they have missed something? Maud couldn't see why Gretel would lie about this, not now.

"But then, who killed—" Maud tripped over the words, almost letting Agatha's name slip. "Then, what happened to the witch?"

Gretel shrugged, apparently more annoyed about Hansel's lie than interested in the mystery. "Who knows? I suppose witches have plenty of enemies."

Maud leaned back against the cart with a thud. Her head was buzzing. Everything that had happened suddenly shifted, dissolving like sugar in water and hardening to create a picture she didn't understand.

None of this made sense.

Mother Agatha didn't have any other enemies, none that Maud had ever heard of. She couldn't imagine who would dislike the kind woman, other than witch hunters. Certainly not enough to push her into an oven.

But that just left Maud with a more pressing question: If Gretel was telling the truth and Hansel hadn't pushed Agatha into the fire, then who, in all the Old Witches' names, had?

10
FORAGING
WITH DRAGONS

The convoy soon moved on, after a very questionable meal of charred veal (Maud thought it was very hypocritical that Wolves accused witches of eating children when they ate *animals*). The novices were still congratulating Hansel for his new initiation and talking excitedly about all the witches they were going to hunt down to earn their own Wolf masks. But Maud barely took any of it in.

She couldn't stop thinking about what Gretel had said.

Only when the cart jerked to a sharp stop did Maud remember that she couldn't risk sitting there lost in thought.

She had to keep her wits around her when hidden among Wolves.

"Foragers!" a voice called.

A boy with deep brown skin, round glasses, and a bag that looked stuffed with either books or bricks jumped to his feet. "Anyone else coming?" he asked, looking around at the blank faces hopefully. He wilted a little as they returned to their conversation.

Maud perked up, interested despite herself. "You go foraging in the Shadelands?"

"Of course," he replied. "We need to eat. And there's lots of interesting things out there."

"Good to find witchbane, I suppose," Maud sighed.

"Not always." He pushed his glasses up his nose. "Personally, I'm interested in moss. I want to collect samples of every variety."

"Moss?" Maud asked, thinking of the Bewitching Hollow and the moss "cakes" still in her pack.

"Yes," he went on eagerly. "All sorts of strange varieties grow in the Shadelands because of the unique ecosystem and the way they have to adapt to the lack of—"

"Foragers!" the voice called again, impatient now. "That means you, Ludo!"

Ludo grimaced. "I better go." He turned to leave, then glanced back at her. "Do you want to come?"

Maud hesitated for a moment. Which was better, foraging with witch hunters or being trapped in a cart with them?

Her legs answered for her, lifting her to her feet. A bit of walking would be good for her, a distraction from this new painful mystery. And she *was* curious about what plants there were in the Shadelands. Besides, she could find some nuts and berries to sneak back to Nuss.

She followed Ludo, Grim nipping at their heels, to a cluster of people all carrying strange, glowing lamps, the same blue hue as the fire. He continued his excited discussion of different types of moss all the way. Maud kept her mouth firmly shut so she didn't accidentally say something about the magical properties of lilac-moss or how the moss in the Bewitching Hollow tasted, in case she gave herself away.

"All right," Rega said to the assembled people. "You know the rules—stick close to the group and don't go outside the circle of light."

None of them looked like warriors of legend now. They weren't even carrying weapons, except for Rega, who had an axe strapped to her back. Maud would've expected all of them to look like the faceless killers she'd imagined. The ones who'd chased her in the wood. But they looked so…ordinary.

"Let's go," Rega finished. She banged a hand on the nearest cart, and the convoy jumped to life again.

Maud's eyes widened. "The convoy's leaving us?"

"No," Ludo replied. "They have to go the long way around. We'll catch up with them when we're done."

Maud followed as the small group of foragers started forward. It really was dark here—darker than the hazy twilight of the convoy—even with the bright blue glow of the lamps. And *quiet* too. A strange kind of quiet that made the hairs on the back of her neck prickle.

"Wait for me!" someone yelled.

Maud's stomach did a backflip. Hansel came hurrying out of the darkness toward them, followed by an annoyed-looking Gretel. So much for being as far from those Wolves as possible.

"Hansel, Gretel," Rega said, "if you want to join us, please be on time."

"Mr. Perfect here couldn't make his mind up," Gretel grumbled.

Hansel waved an apology before grinning at Ludo, all marshmallow lightness. "It's about time I saw all that moss you've been talking about."

Ludo's cheeks pinked a little, and he looked away. "I'm hoping to find some dragon moss today. I think the weather conditions have been correct, and I—"

Maud hurried forward, putting as much space between herself and Hansel as possible. Unfortunately, that meant walking alongside Rega at the front. But, given the possibility of ravaging monsters, being near the person with the large axe was probably a good choice.

Trees crowded in around them. Not trees like Maud was used to, bursting with life and color, but strange, empty ones. Skeletal remains of what had once been called trees.

"Is this the Abandoned Forest?" Maud asked hopefully. Maybe it would be that easy to find the First Witch's spellbook.

"No," Rega said with a chuckle. "You'll know when we reach the Abandoned Forest."

Well, that sounded decidedly ominous.

Trying to think of something else, Maud noticed Rega still wasn't wearing a Wolf mask nor had she congratulated Hansel like so many of the others had.

"Why don't you wear a mask?" The question came out as a squeak, born from Maud having to keep quiet for too long.

Rega's eyebrows twitched, an unamused smile on her mouth. "I'm not a Wolf. Not everyone who travels with the convoy is part of the Wolf Gard."

"The Wolf Gard?" Maud murmured. She'd never heard them called that before.

"That's the official name."

"Oh yes. Of course." Maud quickly cast around for something else to say to cover her mistake. "But I thought everyone here was part of the…Wolf Gard?"

Rega shook her head grimly. "No," she said. "Until recently there weren't even enough Wolves to man a full convoy. They had to bring outsiders too."

Maud opened her mouth to ask why that was, then snapped it shut—she'd already made one mistake, she didn't need to make it more obvious she wasn't meant to be here.

But Rega seemed to read the question from her face anyway. "You're too young to know, but the Wolf Gard only re-formed recently." She jerked her head toward Hansel and Gretel at the back of the group. "Their parents are the Grand Wolves, Hieda and Ermen, the ones who organized it all. My wife and I first led them through the Shadelands years ago, and they still bring me along, even without a Wolf mask."

Maud stared. She wasn't sure which was worse: the fact that Florian was right about Wolves being mostly extinct until recently or that there were people known as Grand Wolves who she could only assume were even worse than these ones.

She still had so many questions, but from the stern way Rega turned her eyes back to their surroundings, Maud took the conversation to be over.

She turned to the strange landscape instead. Maud had foraged a lot before—it was Agatha's favorite chore to assign her—but she had never seen plants like these. Some looked almost familiar, but their colors were off or they were ten times larger than normal ones. She almost tripped over a spiked indigo vine that smelled strangely of burnt sugar, and she passed another that let out hazy clouds of treacle dark vapor.

Maud stopped so suddenly Grim crashed into the back of her legs.

She was staring at some something almost hidden

under a fallen branch. Snow-blossoms, small pink flowers that looked like they'd been dusted in a layer of sugar. Just like the ones that grew around Agatha's cottage. Maud's heart constricted.

Ludo joined her with a low *ooh* of appreciation. "Snow-blossoms," he said. "And in good condition too. That's unusual following the rainy season."

"It reminds me of home," Maud said, her voice very small.

"You should take a cutting of it."

"No, no," Maud said quickly. "I don't want it to die."

"It won't." Ludo reached into his pack and pulled out a small glass tube. "I always look after my cuttings carefully. We'll keep it in water until you can replant it. Then you can carry a piece of home with you."

Maud liked that idea. Gently, she pulled off one of the smaller stems with a few gathered blossoms. Ludo took it with a pair of brass tweezers and nestled it safely into the tube. He added some water, corked the tube and handed it to her, looking pleased.

She squeezed her fingers around it. A little piece of home.

But she'd been so fixated on the flower that she hadn't

noticed the glowing lights of the other foragers had moved much farther ahead. She jumped, about to hurry after them, when she realized Ludo wasn't with her anymore.

She whirled around. He was wandering off in the other direction, toward a patch of rocky moss.

"Ludo!" she called.

"I think this might be it!" he said, not looking back. "The dragon moss, finally!"

"You need to come back!"

But he didn't turn around. The circle of light was drawing farther ahead, the shadows creeping in around Maud like clawed fingers.

And Ludo was getting left behind.

He wasn't her responsibility. And yet…she couldn't just leave him either. Not when all he wanted was to collect a rare moss sample. She could almost hear Florian's admonishing voice. *Don't risk yourself for a witch hunter,* the imaginary vulture said, followed by an equally disapproving, imaginary Nuss: *one less Wolf in the world wouldn't be a bad thing.*

But Grim decided it. He scampered after Ludo without a care in the world.

Maud groaned. She was probably going to regret this. She hurried after them, tripping over the uneven ground in the dark.

Ludo knelt next to a patch of moss. It looked perfectly ordinary to Maud, who was sure she'd been around enough moss the past few days to last her a lifetime, but Ludo grinned up at her.

"It only grows in a place that's been scorched by dragon's fire," he explained excitedly.

Maud touched a finger to it. It seemed to suction on to her like toffee. "It's sticky?"

"Yes," Ludo said. "Dragons also use it to trap their prey."

"Wait," Maud said. "Does that mean—"

A low *screeeech* made her freeze. A dragon emerged from deep within the rocks, its eyes glowing in the thick twilight.

Well, not a full-grown dragon. But even a hatchling was taller than Maud and intimidating enough to make her want to run away.

It didn't look like any of the hatchlings Maud had seen before. She knew there were hundreds of species, ranging from the miniature bumblebee dragons, which buzzed around Agatha's cottage in summer, to flightless wyverns to the amphibian, water-scaled dragons.

But this one felt different. Like the trees, it seemed the Shadelands had changed it. Its wings were a little spikier, its scales a little more ragged, its teeth bigger and sharper. A *lot* sharper.

It didn't look dangerous, though. Curious, more than anything else.

But Maud wasn't planning on taking her chances. Ludo hadn't noticed it, too entranced with his moss find.

"Ludo," she whispered, trying to move her mouth as little as possible.

"Look at the structure of this protonema!"

"Ludo!" she hissed.

He finally looked away from his discovery. "Oh, a dragon," he said, in the same tone someone might say "oh, a stick." Apparently a dragon hatchling wasn't as interesting as moss.

He went back to filling his tiny tube with a sample.

"Ludo," she said again, annoyed at how much she sounded like Florian. "That means we have to go."

Maud had met dragons before. She'd even baked a crème brûlée with one on her eighth birthday (they were very good at the brûlée part). But she wasn't taking risks with any creature in the Shadelands. Especially not a hatchling whose mother could be nearby. Dragon parents were known to scorch first and ask questions later when it came to their hatchlings.

She put a hand on Grim's scruff, pulling him with her. "I think if we just back away slowly, we'll be fine."

Reluctantly, Ludo followed—though not before making sure his sample was safe.

The sharp *snap* of a twig behind her made Maud jump. The dragon hatchling cocked its head.

"Look out!" someone shouted. "There's a beast!"

Before Maud could do anything, before she could even see who had shouted, they leaped in front of her and Ludo with a sword drawn.

The hatchling let out a shriek at the sight of the blade.

But Hansel didn't back down. He brandished the sword as if the little hatchling were a terrible monster.

"Careful!" Maud yelled, grabbing Hansel's arm to give the hatchling time to skitter away. It dove down a small crack in the moss and vanished.

The rest of the foragers followed behind Hansel, their

light suddenly flooding the clearing again. Rega had her axe held aloft.

Hansel turned on Maud. "I almost had it!"

Maud glared at him. "It didn't mean any harm."

"It was going to eat you."

"Why do all of you think you're so appetizing?" Maud shot back. "Not everything wants to eat you!"

Rega stepped forward, cutting Hansel off before he could respond. "You have to stay with the group, remember?" She turned her fierce gaze on Maud. "We can't protect you if you wander off. Ludo, I've told you that before."

There was genuine concern in her voice, like Agatha when she scolded Maud for not being careful with boiling jam. It was odd for someone who traveled with Wolves to remind her of Agatha.

"Sorry," Maud mumbled, though Ludo didn't look very bothered.

"Come on," Rega finished. "Everyone stick together now!"

Hansel glanced back at Maud as they all followed the trail of light back to relative safety. "You could at least say thank you."

"It was a hatchling," Maud said again, fixing him with

her best Florian glare. "Its stomach probably couldn't even handle your head."

Hansel's mouth worked like he was trying to think of a retort, then he gave up. He stalked away, arms tightly folded.

"Thank you!" Ludo called cheerfully to Hansel's retreating back, apparently oblivious to the argument.

Maud didn't say anything. She could feel people watching her. An outburst like that probably wasn't the best way to convince them all that she really was an aspiring witch hunter.

But soon, everyone began to turn their attention away, leaving low buzzes of whispering as they examined their forages. Only Gretel hadn't yet followed the group. She still watched Maud with an odd expression that Maud couldn't quite understand.

"What?" Maud snapped.

Gretel just shrugged. "It's about time someone reminded Hansel he's not a legendary hero."

With that, Gretel marched back to the convoy, leaving Maud thoroughly confused.

11
NETTLES IN
HIS PANTS

When they stopped for the night (though Maud had no idea how they knew it was night, as it looked the same hazy, starless indigo as ever), Maud was relieved to get out of the cramped cart. She'd kept herself folded so tightly into the corner with Grim, determined not to speak to anyone, that all her limbs felt stiff and achy.

Ludo had spent most of the ride despairing over his lost sample, while Oskar laughed at Hansel for not managing to slay a hatchling. As if the poor hatchling had done anything wrong.

At least Maud had her snow-blossoms, tucked safely

with the slightly worse-for-wear gingerbread heart in her pocket.

When they were laying out their bedrolls, Maud took the snow-blossoms out, planning to slip the tube into the blankets for some comfort.

But a hand flashed out and grabbed it before she could do anything.

She spun around to see Oskar and one of the girls sneering at the small blossoms.

"What's this for?" Oskar asked.

"Nothing," Maud said, too quickly.

"Look, Falka," Oskar said, showing the sample to the girl. "We have another botanist like Ludo." He looked back at Maud, a nasty expression on his sour face. "I don't even know why they let him travel with us. Plants and flowers aren't that far from witchcraft."

Maud could feel eyes on her, not just Oskar and Falka but more of the novices, all holding their breath. Waiting to see what would happen.

"I'm not interested in it," she said, her heart accelerating. "It's just a pretty flower, that's all."

Oskar exchanged a look with Falka that made Maud's stomach tighten.

"Then, I suppose you won't mind if I just throw this out?" he asked.

"Of course not," Maud said, wishing her voice wouldn't shake.

Oskar smiled. Very deliberately he dropped the small vial to the ground and stepped on it with one of his massive boots. Maud heard the glass crack, all Ludo's careful work disintegrating.

Oskar stepped back. The snow-blossoms lay ruined in a shower of glass and mud. Any happy memories of Maud's home crushed. Tears stung behind her eyes, but she blinked them away. She couldn't show them how much it hurt.

"Word of advice," Oskar said. "You'll need to be tougher than that to survive out here."

Maud couldn't get to sleep. She kept tossing and turning on the itchy bedroll Rega had given her. But it wasn't really the bed or the constant flickering of those strange torches or the now destroyed snow-blossoms in the mud near her that was keeping Maud up.

She was still thinking about what Gretel had said about Hansel's lie. What it could mean?

When the torch nearest to Maud sputtered out and died, she decided that if she wasn't going to sleep, she may as well do something.

Nuss had been cooped up in the cargo wagon all day, and she was probably hungry enough to begin nibbling on the crates by now. Besides, she could already imagine how grumpy Nuss was going to be at being left alone for so long. Maud shuddered to think what would happen if the squirrel got bored again.

Maud sat up slowly, peering around to see if anyone else was awake. But the whole camp felt still, almost peaceful—which seemed a strange thing to say about a group of bloodthirsty witch hunters. Even Grim was deep asleep, feet in the air and tongue lolling out.

Nudging Grim awake, she stood and picked her way carefully through the sleeping rolls. She almost jumped out of her skin when Oskar rolled over, but he just let out a low snore and settled right back to sleep.

She kept going, squinting in the strange, constant gloom.

She wasn't really doing anything suspicious, she reminded herself, just walking through the camp. If anyone asked, she'd just say she needed to go to the bathroom. That was reasonable enough.

It was almost pitch-black where the cargo wagons were parked on the far edge of camp. Maud could only just pick out faint shapes from the glow of the moon-elks' antlers, grazing quietly nearby.

Luckily, the wagons weren't locked. Maud assumed they didn't expect thieves in the middle of the Shadelands.

The dark inside the cart wasn't much different to the dark outside it, but Maud still couldn't see Nuss. She crept in farther, hoping the floor wouldn't creak.

"Finally!" came a squeaking voice from above her. "I'm about to collapse from starvation."

Maud rolled her eyes. "It's not been that long."

"A long time for a squirrel stomach."

Maud held out the berries she'd saved. "How's this for a squirrel stomach?"

Nuss sniffed them, her nose wrinkled. "I suppose they'll have to do," she said, immediately stuffing three into her mouth at once.

Maud sat down on one of the crates. Being with Nuss again felt so normal amidst all this definite *not* normalness. But that didn't change everything that had happened. After not being able to sleep, Maud suddenly felt exhausted.

"Are you surviving with the witch hunters?" Nuss asked through a mouthful of berries. "They must be awful."

Maud was about to say an emphatic yes, thinking of the novices' jeers and their proclivity for burning witches alive.

But then she thought of Ludo and his love of moss that had nearly got them killed and Rega with her stern kindness.

"They're not entirely horrible," Maud conceded, then realized what she'd said. "Well, some of them, anyway." There were still all the others who were convinced everything wanted to eat them and couldn't wait to kill their first witch.

"One of them scared off a dragon hatchling. And it wasn't even breathing fire yet," Maud added, needing to remind herself that they actually were all that bad. "And another one ruined my snow-blossoms because plants aren't tough and 'witch-huntery' enough."

"You should just put some nettles in his pants," Nuss said matter-of-factly. "Then he'd be too busy itching to be rude."

While Maud had to admit the idea was tempting, it

wouldn't really fit into the whole plan of not drawing attention to herself.

"Or maybe put some flour in their fires." Maud giggled. "That'd put an explosive end to their ridiculous ceremonies."

The laugh caught in her throat as she remembered what she'd learned at that ridiculous ceremony.

"Nuss," she said quickly, "One of the Wolves said they didn't push Agatha into the fire. They said she was already burning when they arrived. But Florian saw the Wolves—he said they did it."

Nuss shook her head. "We didn't actually *see* them. There was someone coming, and Mother Agatha told us to hide. But when we came out, the Wolves were there. It had to be them."

"Maybe not," Maud murmured, her thoughts whirling.

Nuss's chocolate-button eyes widened. "What does that mean?"

Maud shrugged helplessly. She had no idea where to even begin untangling this mess.

They really needed Florian. He'd have some kind of logical answer, even if he said it to them in the most condescending way. Or, even better, Mother Agatha with her calm voice and reassurance that everything would be okay.

But it was just her, Nuss, and Grim stuck in the middle of the Shadelands with one last desperate hope. Tears pricked behind Maud's eyes again.

Nuss nibbled another berry. "They might have been lying."

"I don't think so," Maud replied, swiping at the tears. "They seem to want to show off about hunting witches as much as possible."

"What do you think—"

Shuffling footsteps made Maud slap a hand over Nuss's mouth, sending the berry flying. The squirrel glared, then froze, her ears twitching as she heard the sound too.

In her distraction, Maud had forgotten to keep her voice lowered. Had it attracted something from the Shadelands? A monster or one of the Wolves? She wasn't sure which was worse.

Well, whichever it was, Maud would rather be caught out in the open than in here. There, she could make an excuse to the Wolves and would at least have space to run from any monster.

Grim pressed against her legs, his nose nuzzling as he

tried to hide behind her knees. He really wasn't the most useful of guard dogs.

"You stay here," Maud whispered to Nuss. "And try to be quiet."

Nuss opened her mouth, probably to say loudly that she was always quiet, but when Maud held up a hand, the squirrel relented.

Heart in her throat, Maud slipped back out of the cart and helped Grim down after her. In the hazy shades of dark blue that made up the landscape, Maud couldn't see anything moving. With a sigh of relief, she walked around the edge of the wagon.

And straight into something very solid.

The something solid let out an annoyed huff, stumbling back toward the moon-elk. Their antlers illuminated a short silhouette, framed by two long plaits.

Gretel narrowed her eyes. "What were you doing back there?"

"I was just—" Maud's mind went blank, grasping onto the only vague idea it had "—going to rub some nettles on Oskar's clothes."

For a moment, she wasn't sure how Gretel would react. Would she run and tell one of the adults? Or, worse, Oskar?

It would be better than revealing the truth of what Maud had been doing, but not ideal.

She fidgeted, waiting while Gretel considered her.

"If you really want to annoy him," Gretel said finally, an evil smile spreading across her face, "we should put some in his sleeping bag."

And that was how Maud found herself tramping through weeds and questionable mud in the middle of the night, in the middle of the *Shadelands*, of all places, in the company of a Wolf. Well, a soon-to-be Wolf.

Gretel bent down to examine a spiky plant with red-tipped leaves. "Fire nettles," she said. "Those should do the trick."

"No, they don't really itch too much," Maud said, and pointed at a cluster of yellow nettles a little to their left. "Solnettles will do more." Maud mentally slapped herself. Why was she making this worse? Just get it over and done with as soon as possible.

"Fire nettles sound like they should be worse," Gretel said.

"It's a misnomer."

Gretel shot her a sidelong glance.

Maud looked down, wrapping her hand in her sleeve and then pulling up the solnettles. "Ludo was telling me," she added, hoping it wasn't too obvious she knew far too much about common witch ingredients.

Gretel shrugged. "Come on," she whispered.

Together they crept back through the maze of bedrolls, treading carefully around snoring witch hunters. Luckily, they seemed to be heavy sleepers.

Oskar's bedroll was back near Maud's, between Falka and another novice.

Gretel moved easily through the silence, somehow picking all the quietest spots to place her feet. Maud supposed that was part of their training to make them into even deadlier witch hunters.

Well, she thought, *quiet or not, she still wouldn't outsmart a witch.*

Gretel crouched down by Oskar's bedroll, and Maud followed. Being this close felt like a huge risk, in the midst of all these witch hunters. But at least she would have Gretel to blame. Assuming Gretel didn't blame *her*, of course.

Gretel lifted the edge of Oskar's bedroll and gestured to Maud.

Maud hesitated, one hand holding the solnettles tight.

She could still see the crushed snow-blossoms, hear Oskar's ridiculing tone as he made fun of Grim.

But something about this still didn't feel right.

Florian would definitely tell her this was a bad idea. And what was it Agatha had always said? *You can't fix sour lemon curd by adding more lemon.*

"What're you waiting for?" Gretel hissed, waving her hands toward Oskar.

"Are you sure this is a good idea?" Maud whispered back.

"It was *your* idea."

Maud bit her lip. "But if we do this, then aren't we just as bad as him?"

Gretel gave her an odd, calculating look. It made Maud want to run away—it felt like Gretel could see right through her lies.

But then Gretel just sighed. "I suppose you're not wrong," she conceded, taking a step away from Oskar's sleeping figure. "But only because I want the moral high ground. I still think he's the worst."

"We agree on that," Maud said, before realizing quite what that meant. She'd just said she *agreed* with a witch hunter.

She was so surprised by that realization, by the strange feeling of her and Gretel being on the same side, that she forgot to watch where she stepped as she backed away.

"Hey!" Oskar yelled, sitting up abruptly as Maud's foot came down on his hand.

Maud didn't wait for him to recognize her. He already suspected she was a witch, and this would make it so much worse. She launched herself after Gretel, some of the solnettles flying from her grip in her haste.

"Ouch!" Oskar jumped to his feet, sending more solnettles spraying toward the bedrolls around him. More angry yells burst from the sleepers. All across the camp, Wolves woke up at the commotion with grunts of annoyance or shouts of pain when solnettles made contact with their skin.

"Who did that?" a deep voice yelled as the clamor spread.

Guilt pinched Maud's throat. That was exactly what she'd been trying to avoid. But she couldn't stop now. She and Gretel dove behind one of the carts, taking advantage of the confusion. They were both breathing hard. Maud half expected Gretel to rat her out at any moment.

But instead Gretel shot her a look of sparkling mischief. "You're pretty good at causing chaos, aren't you?"

"I don't mean to."

"Don't worry," Gretel said. "It's a compliment."

Maud's cheeks heated. She was glad it was too dark for Gretel to see. And Maud was too preoccupied with the solnettle damage to stop to figure out *why* a compliment from a witch hunter made her flush.

Out in the camp, the complaints broke off abruptly.

Maud and Gretel peered around the edge of the cart to see two moon-elk canter up to the convoy. Their riders were in clothes so dark they blended with the Shadelands behind them. Their wolf masks made them seem inhuman in the shifting light.

Whispers burst across the convoy, three words that turned Maud's blood cold. "The Grand Wolves."

The moon-elk came to a halt, the towering riders glaring down at everyone. Maud saw Oskar desperately trying to keep still even as solnettle rash erupted on his skin.

"What's going on here?" one of the newcomers asked in a voice that made Maud's stomach flip. "Are you trying to attract every monster in a fifty-mile radius?"

She knew that voice. She knew these Wolves, recognized the dent in the mask where the jar of cinnamon had hit, recognized the gleaming handle of the quartz dagger. These were the hunters she'd seen in the woods by Agatha's cottage.

And, more worryingly, the ones who'd seen *her*.

12
SOME UNCANNY MAGIC

The next morning—Maud was beginning to understand the difference, the slight changes in the darkness—Maud was doing her best impersonation of a shadow. Not literally, sadly. Not just because, as Nuss had pointed out several times, the spell was too hard for her but because there was no way Maud would attempt any kind of magic in present company.

She even appreciated being cramped into the cart near the back with the other novices today. At least it kept a good distance between her and the pair of legendary witch hunters ready to burn any witch they saw at the stake.

The Wolves alone had been bad enough, but now there were *Grand Wolves* here. Rega had called them Hieda and Ermen, the people who had reignited the need to hunt witches. And the ones who had seen Maud before.

If they'd been in the woods that day, there was every chance they'd been in the cottage. Gretel said she and Hansel hadn't attacked Agatha, but their parents could have. Maud could imagine them letting Hansel take the credit. They seemed proud enough of their little would-be murderer.

Everyone else seemed excited by the prospect of the Grand Wolves joining them. In fact, the only other person who looked unhappy was Gretel, which Maud couldn't figure out. And Rega. But Maud was fairly certain Rega's only expression was grumpy.

Oskar couldn't seem to sit still (perhaps solnettle rash lasted longer than Maud had remembered), and as the day went on, his expression got sourer and sourer.

It wasn't helped by Ludo giving a running commentary, alternating between the botanical importance of sol-nettles and various unusual cures Oskar could try.

"I've heard leeches can help with the itching. They might drain your blood too, but—"

"Would you shut up?" Oskar snapped finally. "The nettles were probably your fault anyway."

Ludo's smile evaporated. "How are they my fault?"

"I don't know," Oskar said, evidently happy to have found an outlet for his irritation. "Why would the Wolves bring someone as useless as you along on a mission?"

Ludo ducked his head, saying softly, "I'm not useless."

But the others were joining in now, spurred by the boredom of the long trip.

"Yeah, he's not *useless*," Falka said with a conspiratorial smile. "If we ever get attacked by monsters, he'd be the perfect bait."

Maud gritted her teeth. She shouldn't intervene; she really shouldn't draw attention to herself. Even if it was her fault Oskar was in such a bad mood—her fault they were blaming Ludo.

"The Grand Wolves weren't pleased about the distraction," one of the other boys said. "Maybe we should tell them it was you."

"Then they'd kick you out," Oskar said with relish. "Maybe make you walk back to Gone all on your own. That'd toughen you up."

"Leave him alone." Maud hadn't meant to say it, but the words came bursting out anyway.

They all looked at her, as if suddenly remembering there was other prey in the cart.

"Why're you defending him?" Oskar sneered. "He's never going to cut it as a Wolf. Though, neither are you, I suppose."

Maud's pulse hitched. He didn't know—did he? He couldn't. He was just throwing out insults. But before he had the chance to say anything else, a yell echoed toward them.

"Druden!"

It started as a distant shout, rumbling down the convoy and growing louder and louder as more people took up the cry.

As if they'd trained for this—which, Maud realized, they probably had—the novices all jumped to their feet. As one, they lit the curved torches stationed at the four corners of the wagon. They burned brighter than regular fire, in strange shades of pink and purple. They reminded Maud of beginner cauldron fires.

"Druden?" Maud repeated, half to herself.

"They're nightmare spirits," Ludo supplied, sounding far

more cheerful about those than one should. He nodded to the flickering flames. "Those burn using special minerals. A combination of phosphate and—"

"We don't need a school lesson," Oskar snapped.

Ludo didn't seem to hear him. "—potassium particles at a specific temperature. The druden need pure darkness, so the violet light keeps them away."

Whatever explanation Ludo gave it, the fires seemed like magic. For all the Wolves liked to claim they rejected witchcraft, this wasn't so different. After all, wasn't most magic about combining minerals with a particular intent?

"But we can't burn them all the time," Ludo added. "It'd be a waste."

Oskar glared. "Keep quiet!"

Ludo lowered his voice a fraction but didn't pause in his lecture. "Yes, we need to keep quiet or they might risk the light to try steal—"

"*Ludo!*" the others hissed in unison. Maud got the feeling this was a regular occurrence.

Then, she heard them. Skittering legs like sprinkles over tile and a low rattling hiss that made her stomach curdle. She dug her fingers into Grim's fur, trying to reassure him. He hated strange noises.

"They don't actually eat people, though," Ludo added. "They're scavengers that go after easy prey. So we don't need to worry too much. They're mostly just a nuisance."

Oskar threw something in Ludo's direction. "We don't need commentary from a gatherer. Maybe we should just feed *you* to the druden."

"Oh, leave off, Oskar." To Maud's surprise, it was Hansel who'd spoken. The newly anointed Wolf defending Ludo was certainly not something she'd expected.

Oskar stood up, turning his scowl on Hansel. "Why're you even still here? You're not a novice anymore."

Hansel stood up to match him. "To keep an eye on clod-heads like you."

"*You're* the one causing problems," Gretel grumbled under her breath.

The skittering got louder, the noise crawling up Maud's back, even though she still couldn't see anything in the shadows.

Grim wriggled in her grip, his hackles raised.

"It's okay," she murmured in her best soothing voice.

But the boys were still jostling, and that scrabbling sound was all around them now, the hissing creeping closer.

It all happened too quickly. Oskar lunged at Hansel, top-pling the two of them into one of the torches. It clattered to the ground, its lavender light snuffing out. And Grim jumped right out of her arms, over the side of the cart.

"Grim!" Maud lurched to follow him, but a hand grabbed her arm.

"You can't leave the convoy during a monster sighting," Gretel said, as if that explained everything.

Maud pulled out of Gretel's grip. She leaned over the edge, trying to see Grim in the deep dark. But she might as well have been trying to find a grain of sugar in kraken ink. "We have to go back for him."

Ludo had said the druden were scavengers, only going after easy prey. Well, Grim would be easy prey now, alone and scared in the darkness.

"We can't," Ludo said, his face scrunched with worry. "It's against protocol."

Maud stared at the novices in horror. Even Ludo couldn't meet her eye. She took back every even vaguely nice thought she'd had about the lot of them. They might be fine with the idea of leaving someone behind just because it was against their ridiculous protocols, but Maud wasn't.

She refused to leave anyone else behind.

Without so much as a glance back for permission, Maud grabbed the nearest purple torch and jumped over the edge.

It was a longer drop than she'd anticipated. Her ankle twisted under her as she landed, the torch threatening to fly out of her grip. She only just managed to right it—her lifeline in the darkness.

The convoy pulled on ahead of her, dragging the brighter light with it. After the clashing argument and the eerie skittering, it was suddenly deathly quiet around her. The kind of quiet that might smother her.

She gripped the torch. She didn't have time to be scared. She just had to get to Grim.

Turning on her heel, she tried to remember where in the black landscape Grim had jumped out. "Grim!" she called again, not caring if she attracted monsters. "Here, boy!"

She'd never been in darkness like this. It was thick as molasses and so complete that she could barely tell up from down. She'd only gone two steps when the skittering closed around her again.

She held the torch high. But its soft light barely penetrated the night, let alone illuminate the druden beyond. Not seeing them was somehow worse. Like something constantly lurking behind her. It was making her head spin, cold fear clamming up her throat.

Something scraped across her back, and she whirled around. But all she saw was a skeletal tree, a gaping hollow yawning beneath it like a mouth.

She tried to run back toward where Grim had jumped out, pushing through the licorice dark.

Where was he?

Even if the druden didn't try to pick him off, it would be so easy for Grim to get lost out here. Her heart squeezed. She hated to think of him frightened and alone. "Grim!"

The light caught on a spidery leg, hooked claws glinting purple. Maud stumbled back, the druden gone in the next blink. She hated this. Hated this interminable dark and the isolating fear.

A whimper stood out among the rustling.

"Grim!" she called again. But even with his distant whimpers, she couldn't see where he was. With the shadows and circling nightmares, it was too hard to focus. It was all just too much.

What was it Agatha always told her? *You can't see the way forward if your head's spinning like a top.*

Maud closed her eyes. The Shadelands were confusing

her sight, so she needed to ignore it. To hone in on the thing she could still trust. She let the whispering claws fade to the background and listened for Grim's whimper. *There!*

Hoping there were no more trees—or other creatures—in her path, she shuffled toward the sound, her eyes still tightly closed. She held one hand out, reaching. When she embraced the darkness, it was suddenly so much less confusing.

With a huge wave of relief, her fingers sunk into Grim's coarse lilac fur. Her eyes flew open. Grim pushed up against her with a low snuffle.

She pulled him into a tight hug. "You know I'd never leave you, silly pup."

But she'd been so focused on Grim that she hadn't noticed the skittering. It had risen up around her, tightening closer and closer. In the nearest shadow, a face leaped toward her. Skeletal and clawing, its mouth stretched across its entire skull, jagged fangs bared. Legs—more legs than she could count—stretched out from its neck, covered in hooked claws.

Never mind, she thought. *Maybe I did prefer not seeing them.*

She pulled Grim behind her, wrapping an arm around

him protectively. She swung the torch at the shadow, and the nearest druden lurched back. But one of its crawling claws flicked out. The torch flew from her fingers, and with a sputter, the violet light vanished.

The druden descended at once.

Less substantial than wind, they whirled around her in a storm of nails and teeth. They seemed a little uncertain still. But they'd soon realize she had no light left.

Keeping her head down, Maud ran.

The druden were unrelenting. Their skittering nipped at her heels, hooked claws and fangs reaching toward her. Her heart pounded, her mind losing track of direction again. She couldn't be sure if she was running away from the nightmare creatures or deeper into their midst.

She needed light, but where was she going to find that in this eternal night? She was meant to be a witch, so she should be able to conjure light. Even a cauldron spark would be enough. But she couldn't remember the spell now, panic chasing it out of her head.

The druden were slowly swooping closer, taking their time now. They were pack animals and knew they had their prey cornered. A claw caught her cheek and sent her stumbling.

She steadied herself on the edge of something rough. The tree she'd seen before, with the gaping hollow trunk. Fumbling in the dark, she ducked down to find the space and crawled inside, pulling Grim with her.

It gave her some cover, but she wouldn't be able to outlast the druden. Claws scraped at the bark above her already, sending down showers of splinters.

She grasped the vial around her neck, trying to breathe. If only she had Agatha.

A realization hit her. Agatha might not be here, but Maud did have something of hers. The spellbook.

She pulled it out of her pack, squinting in the darkness. The spells wouldn't be any use if she couldn't read them. She shook her hand, trying to encourage at least a few sparks to see by. Her witchmark prickled, and a tiny burst of light illuminated the book.

She flicked through the pages desperately. There had to be some kind of spell in here that would help. Her pulse was jumping like a rabbit, and the letters swirled, the language of magic more unreadable than ever.

"There!" she breathed. A spell to make daylight. It had more steps than she'd ever seen before and some kind of complicated hand movements, but it was her only chance.

"Mrd—" she tried. *"Mrd-ell…"* But she couldn't get the words to make sense, not like she had that day in the cottage. They spun away, changing with every blink.

"Thgil…" she said, uncertain. *"Emoc ot em!"* She felt the magic that time, but nothing happened.

The few sparks she'd managed to make fizzled out.

With a blood-chilling shriek, the claws ripped through the top of the trunk. In this deeper dark, Maud could see them clearly. A writhing mass, like a shoal of very murderous fish churning above her.

She put herself in front of Grim, bracing for the pain of those claws.

But it didn't come. Instead, a searing light, so bright it burned behind Maud's eyelids, burst all around her.

The druden fled with a shrill hiss, their many legs skittering.

The light winked out. Maud stood up slowly, squinting as flashes still burst behind her lids.

Had she done that?

"Get back!" someone yelled. Where had people come from?

Maud blinked, trying to get her vision to adjust. Smatterings of light still shone in front of her, with people moving between them. The large snake of the convoy had come back. Wolves ran toward her, torches held aloft, as the last of the druden scattered.

Gretel and Hansel led the way, coming to a panting stop next to Maud. Gretel fixed her with a glare. "That was the stupidest thing anyone has ever done."

Maud stuck out her chin. "I wasn't going to lose Grim."

"You might've lost your head."

"Well, I didn't."

Gretel folded her arms. "Only because we came back."

"Isn't that *against protocol*?" Maud asked, raising her eyebrows.

Gretel's scowl deepened. Hansel put a hand on her back. "Everyone's all right," he said. "That's what matters." But that only seemed to make Gretel more annoyed.

The Wolves were closing in around her, all marveling at their triumph over the druden. No one had mentioned the bright burst of light that Maud might or might not have conjured. Maybe she was still safe.

"Who did that?"

Just like last night, that cool voice sliced through the air. Everyone fell silent, stepping back to allow the Grand Wolves through. They were both looking right at Maud.

She squirmed, trying for her innocent voice. "Did what?" It came out closer to Nuss's guilty squeak when she'd left paw prints in the raincloud jam.

"That light," Ermen spat. "That was *magic*."

"I think it was one of our flash blasters," Hansel said, a little uncertain in front of his parents. "We have lots of—"

Hieda took a deliberate step forward. "No," she said. "I know a witch's work when I see it."

Her eyes lowered to Maud, to the heavy tome Maud hadn't realized was still clutched in her hands. Agatha's spellbook. Her stomach lurched.

There was nowhere for Maud to hide, no way to conceal the bulk of the book. She wrapped her arms around it, hoping to at least cover the title.

"M-magic?" she stammered as Hieda advanced. "I don't know what you mean. I'm a novice. I hate magic and all things witchy—"

Before Maud could finish her somewhat unconvincing speech, Hieda wrenched the book from her grasp. She flipped through it with a disgusted curl to her lip, as if it were a curdled batch of buttercream, not Maud's most prized possession.

Maud wanted to snatch it back, to hold it close. But

there were Wolves all around, and they were beginning to look at her with suspicion.

"That's not mine," Maud tried again. "I just found it..."

Hieda raised her eyebrows. "And I suppose we won't find a witchmark on you?"

Maud took a step back, unable to stop her left hand from twitching toward her right. Telling Hieda exactly where to look.

Hieda grabbed her wrist. She pushed up Maud's tattered sleeve to reveal the crescent moon that marked Maud as a witch. There was no denying that.

Low gasps ran through the group, more chilling than the rustle of the druden.

"A little witchling." Hieda smiled, but there was no humor there. "Hiding among us."

Maud tried to pull back, but Hieda's grip was immovable. Spread out behind Hieda, the faces of the people Maud had come to know these past few days morphed into unfamiliar masks. No matter the small kindnesses some of them had shown her, every one of them was a witch hunter.

And she was trapped.

A squawking yell cut through the air. A very familiar squawking yell.

The Wolves all turned to the source of the commotion. With a spluttering hiss, one of the carts erupted into flames. In the same instant, a small explosion of mousse and chocolate launched itself at Hieda.

The witch hunter released Maud, swiping at the squirrel now clinging to her hair. The rest of the Wolves scattered. Ermen lunged toward Maud while the others hurried to put out the fire.

Maud threw the nearest thing she had to a weapon. Agatha's spellbook cracked Ermen on the head, and Maud dodged around him. Still wrestling with Nuss, Hieda stumbled back and tripped over the thick tree roots. She hit the ground with a low *oof*.

Maud took her chance. She snatched up Nuss, called for Grim to follow, and sprinted as fast as she could. Away from the light of the burning cart and the moon-elk and into the dark abyss of the Shadelands.

13
THE DARKEST PLACE

Maud's lungs were burning, but she kept on running. The shouts of the Wolves and glow of their torches had long since faded away, but still Maud couldn't stop. Some of them might be distracted by their now-burning supplies, but it would take just one of them catching up for this to all be over.

Only when Grim let out a low snuffle of discomfort did Maud finally slow down. She bent down next to the wolf pup, checking for any signs of injury.

"You okay?" she murmured, stroking his shaking ears. "Good boy. Such a good Grim. We're safe now."

Though Maud was pretty sure that wasn't true. In fact, this might be the furthest from *safe* she'd ever been.

Nuss hopped down from her shoulder and up onto a tree stump with a look of deep offense. "I'm fine, too, you know."

"I do know," Maud shot at her. "Because if you weren't fine, you'd very vocally let me know."

Nuss sniffed, turning her back to Maud to fully demonstrate her annoyance.

"It'd be your fault anyway if you weren't," Maud said. "You're the one who thought it was a great idea to start a fire and then launch yourself at a Grand Wolf."

Nuss primly picked a twig from her tail. "If I hadn't, we'd still be trapped back there."

"Don't pretend you thought it through," Maud replied. "We both know you just like setting things on fire."

"If it works, it works."

"Anyway," Maud added, "that whole argument started because of you and that stupid nettle idea."

Nuss raised her paws. "I didn't make you do that. I just happened to have an excellent suggestion."

Maud slumped down on a log, dropping her head in her hands. Nuss was right. Nuss always had some harebrained scheme; that didn't mean Maud had to go along with it. She'd let herself get too comfortable, forgetting the real danger. And the real reason she was here.

Now she'd lost Agatha's spellbook—a loss that burned in her stomach—and the map. Not to mention the protection of the convoy. Maud was out in the Shadelands on her own, without any idea how to find the Abandoned Forest or the spellbook within.

Maud jolted back to her feet with a gasp. She'd been so focused on running, on making sure Grim was all right and arguing with Nuss, that she hadn't noticed what was all around them.

Trees.

Not the few skeletal trunks that had been scattered around before, but *actual* trees. Well, not quite trees as Maud had seen them before.

They were massive. At least three times as tall as the trees in the wood by Agatha's cottage, with trunks so wide several people could stretch their arms around them. But that wasn't the only thing that made them unusual.

Thick veins of pale blue and silver pulsed through them like blood. Heavy fruit hung from some in a cascade of strange colors, while others were adorned with spiked flowers, edges gleaming like knives, or acorns as dark as the night sky and emitting a faint hum.

"This is it," Maud said, her voice coming out in a hushed whisper. "*This* is the Abandoned Forest."

Nuss wrinkled her nose. "Does it seem abandoned enough?"

"I think there's only the one forest of giant trees that lives in eternal darkness."

And it wasn't just that. Maud knew all trees were living things, but these somehow seemed *more*. Not just growing and flowering, but watching. Waiting for something.

Nuss gazed up at the expanse of the forest. "But it's huge. How will we find the First Witch's book?"

Maud didn't have an answer to that.

The map was still somewhere back at the convoy along with Agatha's spellbook. She wouldn't be able to get them back now. All those spells so carefully written in Agatha's hand, collected over so many years. And they were gone.

Just like Agatha. And Florian, who Maud was afraid they'd never find again. Then she'd almost lost Grim too.

Then there was the legion of witch hunters on her tail. She imagined it was only the surprise—or maybe Maud's lack of importance as a fledgling—that had allowed her to escape them in the first place.

So now Maud was in the middle of a monster-filled forest, being chased by Wolves, with nothing but some ashes and a bag of useless ingredients, plus two vulnerable creatures she had to protect.

She didn't want to lose them too. She wasn't sure how much more she *could* lose before she began to crumble away.

Maybe this was all just too much for her. A witch made of gingerbread who couldn't even do basic spells. Maybe she should've just stayed in the cottage and given up. Let them all turn back into nothing but crumbs.

No. Maud's jaw clenched. A steely determination clamped around her. She might be able to give up on herself, but she refused to give up on the others.

She got to her feet. "Right," she said with as much confidence as she could muster (she hoped if she sounded confident enough, maybe she could make it true). "We found the forest. How hard can it be to find a spellbook?"

She knew from the way Nuss was nibbling on her bottom lip that the answer was "very hard," but Maud couldn't let even a shred of confidence go or she'd definitely give up.

"We could try a Toadstool Path?" she wondered aloud.

"Would that even work out here?" Nuss asked. "I don't see any toadstools."

"Okay…" Maud looked around, as if the dark trees might provide some answer. "What about breadcrumbs? I think I still have some left and I remember that spell."

"Except that you need to know what you're looking for," Nuss reminded her. "And we've never seen the spellbook."

Maud pressed her lips together. She refused to let her confidence waiver.

What had she done before when she'd been stuck? She'd always had Agatha or Florian, of course, to nudge her in the right direction. To help her see through the confusion to the simple solution she'd missed.

Maybe that was it. She just needed a simple answer.

"What was it Vira said about where the spellbook was buried?"

Nuss rubbed her chin. "Uhh…something about a hidden glade."

"In the darkest part of the forest," Maud finished.

She looked to her left, then her right, then her left again.

Running all that time in the endless night had given her eyes a chance to adjust. Away from the Wolves' torches she could see the Shadelands weren't really just a mass of darkness. There were subtle hues to it: bright licorice black fading to the soft indigo of blueberries.

And to her right was definitely darker than to her left.

Nuss crawled up her arm to settle on her shoulder. "I hope this is an actual plan now."

"*Plan* is a big word," Maud said, "but I have an idea. And I'm pretty sure it's right."

Without waiting for any more of Nuss's complaints, Maud turned to her right and walked toward the deeper darkness.

14
FRIEND
OR FOOD

It didn't take long for the treacle black to close around them. But it didn't scare Maud, even as Nuss's claws dug into her shoulder. Because Maud thought she understood something about the forest and its watching trees now. The thicker the darkness became, the closer she was to her goal.

Almost like it was helping her find the way.

A noise from behind made her jump, nearly dislodging Nuss.

"Wolves or monsters?" Nuss whispered as Grim pressed close to her calf.

Maud wasn't sure which was worse.

"Let's just keep going," she murmured back, helping Grim over a tree root taller than him.

The noise had seemed far enough away, and she couldn't see any sign of the telltale pricks of light the Wolf Gard brought with them.

Though a monster wouldn't carry light to warn her. And this far into the Shadelands, there'd be far worse than druden.

She took a breath, shaking her head to dispel her worries. There was no point in turning back now, so they had to forge on.

More sounds rustled around them the farther they walked. Soft noises that seemed to suit the forest—definitely not the clattering of Wolves. Maud caught snatches of scaled wings overhead and slithering tails in the undergrowth. But the creatures didn't seem particularly interested in her.

Just like with the beasts in any wood—if she didn't bother them, they probably wouldn't bother her. The theory seemed to hold, anyway.

Further proof that most creatures weren't out to eat humans, despite what the Wolves said. Maud couldn't imagine humans would taste very nice anyway. Very stringy and unseasoned.

But Nuss didn't seem to agree with that line of thought. She kept up a running commentary of the various things she was convinced would attack at any moment.

"What if we run into the mossfolk?" Nuss whispered in Maud's ear. Talk of moss made Maud think of Ludo. He'd probably love to meet the mossfolk.

"They could hypnotize us," Nuss went on. "Or there might be a nixe that wants to drown us."

"We're nowhere near water," Maud pointed out.

"A night raven, then," Nuss pushed on, undeterred. "They've got giant wings and hooked claws specially for tearing out hearts."

Maud sighed. She really shouldn't have let Nuss read that book on night creatures last solstice.

"Or maybe—"

Maud stopped so suddenly Nuss almost fell off her shoulder.

A sound, much closer than any of the others, reverberated against the massive trunks. The ghostly echo of a bird's hunting cry.

"Night ravens!" Nuss blurted.

"No," Maud said, though she wasn't so sure now. This wasn't the small natural sounds of the forest. This was the sound of something hunting. The silence suddenly seemed to magnify around her, not true silence at all. Claws skittering over wood, another echoing cry, the slithering of something over leaves.

Maybe Maud had been wrong to trust the forest was leading her in the right direction. Perhaps it had just been luring her in deeper to devour her.

She let out a snort of laughter. Now she was sounding like one of the Wolves, convinced everything wanted to eat her. Forests certainly didn't eat people.

Crunch.

Maud froze. She turned around slowly. She could just make out a shadowy shape moving between the trees behind them.

She scurried out of its path, pulling Nuss and Grim down into a small hollow hidden by giant overhanging roots. Whatever it was, she didn't think it had seen them yet. No sense in running and alerting it to their presence.

"Do you think it wants to steal our hearts?" Nuss squeaked.

Maud put a finger to her lips. *Quiet.*

She didn't point out that of the three of them, only Grim had a real heart to take anyway.

A rattling chill spread over her skin. A presence reaching toward her, unhindered by her hiding place. She glanced up and could see the edge of an inky talon, slick and sharp.

Just stay still, she told herself. *Don't provoke it, and it'll leave.*

She was so still she wasn't breathing. After a few stumbling heartbeats, the presence receded, as if another scent had caught its interest.

"What was that?" Nuss whispered, peeking around the roots.

"I know you're down there, witch!"

Maud was so surprised to hear a human voice she almost laughed. That was definitely better than whatever that cold presence had been. She clamped her hand over her mouth to stifle the sound.

Wolves were still dangerous.

Someone jumped down in front of them.

For a moment, it was just the dark silhouette of a Wolf towering over her, Maud cornered and at its mercy. Then the intimidating shadow shifted into a familiar figure.

"I told you I knew you were there," Gretel said, raising her wolf-handled sword.

There was a strange disconnect. The moments Maud and Gretel had smiled together blurring with the murderous Wolf in front of her.

When Maud had imagined the Wolves following her, they'd been faceless. Just those inhuman masks. She hadn't expected it to be Gretel. And Maud hadn't realized how much that would hurt. Gretel had come back for her and Grim. She'd made Maud forget that she was a witch and Gretel was a hunter.

But apparently even knowing each other didn't change that.

Nuss let out a not-very-intimidating growl.

Gretel raised her eyebrows. "What is that?"

"Why does everyone keep asking that?" Nuss huffed.

Gretel recoiled a little. "It talks?"

Maud stepped forward slowly, intervening before Nuss could start an argument. "I don't want any bother," she said, opting to try the same approach as with the night creatures. Gretel hadn't seemed quite as eager for a witch's blood as the others. Maybe this didn't have to get any worse. Didn't have to force them to be enemies. "I'll just keep going on my way and leave you alone."

But Gretel's sword blocked her path. "I'm hunting you," she said, as if Maud were very dense. "You have to come with me."

Maud glared. "Why?"

Gretel blinked back at her, confused.

"Why?" Maud asked again. "What did I ever do to you?"

"You infiltrated our mission. Probably because you wanted to learn our secrets and destroy us."

Maud sighed. "I never wanted to end up in your convoy. That was an accident."

"You should come up with a better lie than that," Gretel said, sounding very like her mother.

"I didn't do anything, though, did I? I didn't hurt anyone." Maud bit her lower lip. "Well, maybe a bit with the solnettles, but that was you too."

Gretel stuck out her chin. "That's not the point."

"Then, what is?"

"You're a witch."

"So, that's it?" Maud asked. "You hunt people just because of how they're made—born," she amended quickly. "How they're born."

Gretel gave her an odd look. Then she went back to her glower. "I'm capturing a witch," she said, though Maud thought she could hear a slight hesitation. "That's more than Hansel managed. And that's what matters."

Maud opened her mouth to respond, when that creeping cold came back. A presence, like eyes on the back of her head. A hollow screech whirled around them, more solid than a sound should be.

Maud whipped around to see something sweeping down on them.

"Night raven!" Nuss squeaked. This time Maud didn't disagree.

Taller than an adult, the creature towered over them. Its wings were spread wide, each feather the length of Maud's arm and the shiny black of currants. Its beak was hooked and razor sharp, sitting between two milk-white eyes. Those gleaming talons did look ready to tear out their hearts.

Or, they would if Maud *had* a human heart.

"Don't move." Maud forced herself to stay still even as her mind screamed at her to run. That would make them look like immediate prey.

Gretel ignored her and took a step forward.

"*Don't*," Maud said again. "If you don't attack, it might just ignore us."

Gretel raised her sword, her face set. It might've been brave if it weren't so incredibly stupid.

The night raven lunged.

Maud dove to the side, pulling Grim with her, and crashed into the uneven ground. But Gretel swung her sword to meet the creature. The blade clanged against its beak as if it were also made of metal.

Maud scrabbled to her feet, looking between the dark safety of the trees at her back and the night raven in front of her.

Nuss tugged on her hair. "What're you waiting for? Run!"

They could run. The night raven was too focused on Gretel to follow. And Maud didn't owe the witch hunter anything. Gretel had already said she planned on taking Maud back to the Wolves as a captive. Besides, Gretel seemed to have it under control, ducking and weaving around the night raven's attacks with ease.

Maud took a tentative step back. She didn't want to attract any attention. When neither the giant bird nor the witch hunter so much as glanced at her, Maud hauled herself over a twisting tree root and prepared to run. Nuss scrabbled with her, squeaking encouragement.

A heavy thump made her look back. The night raven had Gretel pinned with a single, gleaming talon. As Maud watched, it plucked Gretel's sword from her grip and threw it aside to leave her defenseless.

Maud's heart sank.

It was just like when Ludo had wandered off after the moss, but Grim wouldn't make the decision for her this time.

Nuss dug her claws into Maud's shoulder. "Maud!" The squirrel nudged. "Time to go!"

Maud let out a huff of annoyance. She was going to regret this.

She reached into her pack and grabbed something at random. "Hey!" she yelled, but the night raven didn't look up. She threw the object. "Birdbrain!"

The random object—a small jar of pickled beetle legs, by the looks of it—smashed over the creature's oil-slick feathers.

It let out an angry screech, turning its cloudy eyes on her.

Yep, Maud definitely regretted that.

She felt its creeping presence reach for her again. Then the creature spread its wings wide and swept toward her.

Maud didn't have time to dive out of the way. She didn't even have time to be afraid. The edge of the night raven's great wing smashed into her shoulder, sending her crashing back into a gnarled root. The fall knocked the air from her lungs, and lights burst in her vision.

She struggled to catch her breath as the night raven advanced. How was she meant to fight this? She couldn't even begin to think of a spell that might help, let alone one she could *do*.

Desperate, she reached into her pack again. Pulling out the first thing she grasped, she threw it at the bird. Slimy frogspawn burst on the night raven's wing. It hardly seemed to notice.

Its head swayed, as if it was looking for her in the dark. That creeping chill reached for her again, clammy against her skin.

Nuss was pulling on her arm, and Grim was whimpering, but Maud couldn't drag enough air into her lungs to get her legs to move.

The night raven loomed over her. Its head dipped, almost like it was smelling her. It began to pull back, preparing to strike.

She grasped for something—anything—that might

work as a weapon. Her fingers clenched around another vial, and she threw it. Probably making a mess more than achieving anything.

It hit the night raven square between the eyes. The jar exploded in a shower of glass and pale beige powder—nutmeg or maybe ginger? The creature reared back, something flickering in that space between its eyes. The cold presence receded with it.

Gretel had retrieved her sword and tried to swing at the night raven again. The bird thrashed wildly, its wings flailing wide.

Maud hauled herself to her feet—only for one of those wings to catch her on the side. It sent her and Gretel tumbling back into one of the trees. Maud's foot slipped into a small cavity. She kicked at the loose bark, revealing a hole at the base, just wide enough for her shoulders.

One of the night raven's talons slammed into the tree above Maud's head. It gouged a deep gash. She didn't like to think what that would've done to her flesh.

"In here," she whispered, pushing Nuss and Grim into the safety of the trunk. She crawled in after, relieved to find the space was big enough for all of them. "Come on," she hissed to Gretel.

Gretel looked back at the careening bird and its flailing talons. She seemed to be weighing her dislike of being anywhere near a witch with her likelihood of survival. Self-preservation won out, and Gretel clambered in after her.

The night raven crashed into the tree again, shaking it right down to the roots. It seemed to be trying to get the nutmeg out of its feathers.

"What now?" Nuss asked.

"I think it's blind," Maud whispered. "And it uses some sort of magic to sense us."

"How does that help us?" Gretel panted.

"I saw a kind of third eye when I hit it with the nutmeg. I think we could use that to confuse it."

Gretel raised her sword hopefully. "Okay, so I stab it be-tween the eyes."

Nuss pushed the sword point away from her nose with a grumble of annoyance.

"Stabbing things doesn't solve every problem," Maud said.

"It solves *most* problems."

Maud ignored her. She twisted in the cramped space to open her pack, choosing with intent this time. Pepper-corn powder. "I think this will do it."

162

She'd once accidentally inhaled some pure peppercorn powder when making warm spiced bread and her eyes had streamed for hours.

"You distract it," Maud said. "And I'll come up behind with this."

"Why don't you be the distraction?"

Maud couldn't say the truth: *I'm made of gingerbread, and the monster seems more interested in beating hearts.* So she just said, "Would you rather face the night raven with a sword or with some spices?"

The answer was clear on the witch hunter's face.

"Fine," Gretel grumbled. "But we go on my count. Three, two, one…" She took a deep breath. "Go!"

Gretel charged out of the hole first, brandishing her sword as Maud scrambled after her.

Gretel's wild battle cry drew the night raven's attention. It seemed to have regained its balance, the nutmeg cleared from its third eye. Maud tried to keep behind the creature—away from its strange magic sensors—but she was pretty sure it was most interested in Gretel and the direct threat of that sword.

"That's right!" Gretel yelled. "Come get me!"

The night raven obliged. It let out a piercing hunting

cry, rearing up with its huge wings spread, and struck. It moved faster than Maud's eye could follow. A sharp blur of feathers and talons. Pinning Gretel easily, its serrated claws dug into her shoulder until blood beaded.

"Anytime now!" she yelled at Maud.

But Maud couldn't rush. If she moved too fast or posed herself as a threat, the night raven would sense her.

I'm nothing but gingerbread, Maud thought, trying to project her most not-alive self. The opposite of what she usually did.

The talons pressed deeper, and Gretel let out a low grunt of pain. "Maud!" The sharp beak dipped toward her, and Maud could almost hear the witch hunter wondering if she should have put her trust in a witch.

But Maud always stuck to her word. And she wasn't leaving anyone behind. Even her mortal enemy.

She lunged forward. Pulling out the stopper, she closed her eyes and threw the peppercorn at the space between the night raven's eyes.

Maud definitely saw its third eye now. A flutter as dark as the feathers around it, already streaming where the peppercorn hit. The night raven let out another screech and reeled back, sending Gretel flying.

It swung its head back and forth, floundering. Off-balance, it staggered a few steps, then spread its wings and took off in a lurching flight.

With its senses disrupted, it kept veering into branches, leaving a trail of broken twigs in its wake.

Gretel stared after it. "Pity I don't have a bow and arrow."

"You don't have to kill everything you don't like," Maud said. She bit her lip, watching the night raven vanish into the dark. "I hope I didn't do any permanent damage."

"It just tried to kill us," Gretel said from the bush she'd landed in.

Maud shrugged, holding out a hand that Gretel ignored. "Everything needs to eat, doesn't it? And anyway, you attacked first."

Gretel heaved herself upright, that odd look on her face again. "You're a very unusual witch, you know."

Maud let out a laugh. Gretel didn't know the half of it.

Gretel cocked her head. "Why didn't you run when you had the chance?"

Maud opened her mouth to reply, but wasn't quite sure she could put the tangled answer into words.

A spatter of rain fell from the sky. It splashed between

Maud's feet, thick as toffee. As if it had been waiting for a cue, a torrent of raindrops followed.

Any answer died in her throat. She met Nuss's chocolate eyes. Rain. *Water.* She clenched her fingers around the vial of ashes.

"Quick!" Nuss said. She tore a piece of cloth from Maud's shirt with her sharp claws and wrapped it around the vial.

"I could've just put it in my pocket," Maud said, poking the new hole in her shirt.

"What is—" Gretel started to ask, but her words slurred away. A dark patch stained her shoulder—not from the rain but from where the night raven had grasped her.

Maud stepped forward. "Are you all right?"

Gretel waved her off. "I'm perfectly fine."

But Maud could see the wound, black veins spreading from it. She glanced at Nuss. "Do you remember reading about night ravens being poisonous?"

"It's nothing," Gretel said again. "I've had far worse than this before."

She'd barely finished the sentence before she collapsed to the ground.

15
WITCHES DON'T EAT CHILDREN

"Gretel!" Maud cried, kneeling next to the witch hunter. Maud shook her, and Gretel's eyes fluttered. At least she was alive. But black was spreading from Gretel's shoulder through the rest of her veins.

Maud didn't know much about venom—definitely not night-raven venom—but that didn't look good.

Cold panic threatened to take over. Too many options burst in her head, holding her in place like a freezing spell.

The rain was falling harder now. Pounding drops as thick as tree sap. She couldn't risk even a trickle of water on the ashes, and she couldn't concentrate with that hanging over her head. *One thing at a time*, she told herself. Just like any recipe, you can't think about step twelve when you're only just preparing the ingredients.

So step one: get out of the rain.

She put her arm under Gretel's shoulder and pulled her up. "Can you walk?" she asked. "We need to find shelter. Then I can try help." She wasn't sure how true that was, not with half her supplies missing and Agatha's spellbook long gone, but she wasn't going to say that.

Gretel nodded, her eyes unfocused.

Maud tried to walk, but with Gretel's added weight and Nuss's fidgeting, she kept tripping.

They couldn't go back into that tree. Riddled with talon holes, it would soon fill with water—and water was not Maud's friend right now. But where else was there to hide in this forest?

She stumbled forward, squinting in the rain and shadows. There was something up ahead of her, almost as if the forest had been listening.

A faint light flickered through the trees. As they got closer, Maud could make out a quaint stone cottage, thin plumes of periwinkle smoke rising from the chimney.

"A witch's cottage," Maud said in relief at the same moment Gretel hissed, "A witch's den."

"We'll be safe in there," Maud assured her. "Witches always look after their own."

Gretel shook her head. "Not me."

Nuss grimaced, eyeing Gretel's wolf-handled sword. "Maybe we should leave that out here." She scuttled down and grabbed the hilt, tipping it to the ground.

Gretel attempted to go back for it, but her movements were getting weaker. "She'll eat us," she mumbled.

"Witches don't eat people," Maud said for what felt like the millionth time. Granted, she'd never heard of witches living in the Shadelands—let alone all the way in the Abandoned Forest. But witches always stuck to their code; the Witching Guild made sure of it.

The cottage would have all the ingredients she needed to help Gretel, and they were both shivering with cold. That fire looked very tempting.

"It's the cottage," she told Gretel. "Or take your chances out here with another night raven."

Gretel let out a grumbled noise that sounded something like "I'd rather do that," but Maud took it as agreement.

It was difficult work getting Gretel up the front path,

especially with rain slicking the stone cobbles. The witch hunter was taller and Maud's muscles were shaking to keep them both upright. Nuss scampered ahead, her tail twitching as she examined the gleaming green door. It was bright and clean and out of place in this forest.

"You could help," Maud said to the squirrel.

Nuss shrugged. "You're the one who insisted on bringing the Wolf along." She put an ear to the door. "I don't hear anyone."

Maud heaved Gretel the last few paces and reached for the brass knocker, which was shaped like a wreath of leaves. No one answered.

"Hello?" Maud called.

Still nothing.

She leaned over to peer through the square window, framed by a neatly painted trellis. Though a fire burbled happily in the hearth, the cozy room looked empty of people. Maybe the witch was out gathering supplies?

Tentatively, Maud pushed on the door. It swung open, letting out a wave of welcome warmth.

"I'm sure they won't mind if we just warm ourselves for a while," Nuss said, already hopping over the threshold.

Gretel seemed too delirious to disagree, which was enough of an answer for Maud.

Inside was bright and warm and smelled just liked Agatha's cottage did on a winter day, that scent of wood smoke and cloves. It sent homesickness curling through Maud's stomach. She so wished she was back there. Back where she didn't have to worry about everything. Back where she was safe.

Maud squeezed her eyes shut, a few tears seeping out. It shouldn't be long now. They couldn't be far from the First Witch's spellbook this deep into the forest. She'd managed step one: get out of the rain. Now she just needed step two: heal Gretel so that she wasn't left wandering injured through this forest. Then, step three: wait out the rain and go find the spellbook.

It sounded simple enough when she put it like that.

She settled Gretel and Grim under a soft quilt by the fire, then she and Nuss got to work in the kitchen. Maud didn't know much about poisons, but Agatha had taught her one basic antidote: a cureall.

Nuss let out a disapproving sniff as she fetched one of the copper pots hanging on the wall. "I still don't see why you brought the Wolf with us."

"I'd never leave Grim."

Nuss narrowed her eyes. "You know what I mean."

Maud took the pot from her and set about preparing the ingredients. She did know what Nuss meant. It was the same thing Gretel had asked before she collapsed. But Maud still didn't have a good answer, other than it had felt wrong to abandon the witch hunter. Even if Maud wasn't sure Gretel would have done the same if their situations had been reversed.

The kitchen was well stocked with everything a young witch could possibly need, from upside-down mushrooms and boiled frogspawn to things Maud had never even heard of before, like extract of a baby's laugh and essence of a sunflower's tears.

The cureall was quick and easy to make, more a concoction than an actual spell as no magic was required. Agatha always had a jar handy in case any of them got into a scrape. Which they always did. So she made a new batch pretty much every week.

Maud sprinkled on the last of the dawn dewdrops and gave it a final stir. She poured the pale blue liquid into a cracked mug.

Gretel was a little more awake when Maud brought her

the cureall, perhaps revived by the warm fire. She had one hand curled in Grim's fur, though Maud had a feeling that wasn't intentional. She doubted Gretel would willingly touch a creature associated with a witch.

"Here," Maud said, holding out the mug.

Gretel took it with a suspicious sniff. "What is it?"

"Cureall," Maud replied. "It should make you feel better."

"We hope," Nuss added helpfully. "Unless night-raven venom is immune to it."

Gretel swirled the mug with deep uncertainty. "Is it magic?"

"No," Maud said, sitting cross-legged on the rug opposite her. "It's medicine."

Nuss curled in front of the fire, preening her tail. "We could always let the venom kill you," she said, sweet as honey. "We wouldn't mind."

Gretel shot Nuss a look, then sipped the cureall. When she didn't immediately choke, she took a longer drink.

"Better than you expected?"

"Not bad," Gretel conceded, "for something made by a witch."

"Right." Maud scooted back, wrapping her arms around

her knees. For some people, she wouldn't ever be enough of a witch, and for others she'd always be too much.

The cottage was filled with nothing but the sound of crackling wood and Nuss cleaning her tail.

Gretel was watching Maud over the rim of the mug. "If you weren't trying to infiltrate our ranks," she said, "then, what were you doing?"

Maud opened her mouth, then shut it. She didn't even know where to begin with that. "I needed to come into the Shadelands."

"Because it's such a fun holiday destination?"

Nuss looked up with a glare. "Because you pushed Mother Agatha into the oven."

You could always count on Nuss to bring the blunt truths.

Gretel blinked, glancing from the squirrel to Maud. Maud could almost see the pieces falling into place in the witch hunter's mind.

"That house made of gingerbread," Gretel said slowly. "The one where Hansel claimed his first witch hunt."

Maud nodded, not sure if she could speak.

"Why did that mean you had to travel to the Shade-lands?"

Maud's fingers closed around the vial of ashes, safe and dry in the folds of her clothes. She wasn't going to share that secret. Gretel seemed to have decided she wasn't going to try drag Maud back to the Wolf Gard, but that didn't mean she could trust her.

"To find a way to bring her back," Nuss said.

"Nuss!" Maud hissed. "That was not information to be shared."

"I mean," Nuss amended, far too late, "none of your business."

"We thought she was a witch," Gretel said quietly.

"She was a witch."

Gretel squeezed the mug. "The bad kind."

"Well," Maud said, her eyes burning at the thought of anyone calling Agatha a bad witch, "she wasn't."

Maud expected Gretel to press the point, but she didn't say anything. She was watching the fire, perhaps wondering if she should try push Maud in.

Gretel drained the last of the cureall, some color finally coming back to her cheeks. "Thanks," she said, very quiet.

"Thanks?"

"Yeah, for saving me."

"I still think she should've left you to the night raven," Nuss said.

Gretel put the mug down. "Why didn't you?"

That question again. Maud shrugged. "Even hunters are people. Just like there can be good and bad witches. I suppose there can be good and bad hunters."

"What if I still tried to capture you?"

Maud gestured to Gretel's shoulder. "You're not in much state to capture anyone."

"But I wanted to," Gretel said. She looked down. "And I probably should still try. That's what my parents would tell me to do."

Maud put her chin on her knees. "You don't always do what they tell you. You didn't tell them about the nettles."

Gretel shook her head. "That was unusual. You know my parents are the Grand Wolves."

Maud nodded, trying not to remember Hieda and Ermen and their terrifying presence.

"Well, Hansel and I were expected to live up to that," Gretel went on. "Hansel's always been the golden boy who could do nothing wrong. So I had to work twice as hard. Be twice as good a hunter. He didn't even complete his first hunt properly, and they still initiated him." She glanced up with a slight grimace. "Sorry."

Maud understood that feeling. The painful need to prove herself and yet never quite being enough.

"And it's more than that," Gretel said. "They made the Wolf Gard what it is today. It's not just a job to them, it's a way of life. A way to get vengeance for the terrible acts of the Crimson-cloaked Witch who murdered our ancestors."

Maud frowned. "I've heard that story a little differently."

Gretel shrugged, her eyes lowered. "I suppose they might not be right about everything." She gestured to Maud. "You did save me, so you're not *entirely* evil."

"And I suppose you're not either," Maud admitted. "You came back for me and Grim, even if it was against protocol."

Gretel made a face. "But being a Wolf is all they ever wanted for me. All that mattered to them was growing our ranks again. So that's all I worked for, all I let myself want. But now I don't even know what that means anymore."

"What do you really want?"

Gretel shook her head again, looking a little lost. "I don't know."

A twinge went through Maud's gut. For all of her fears,

for all her doubts and annoyance at not being allowed to learn magic, at least she had always known what she wanted. Even if it felt impossible at times, she had that to hold on to.

What would it be like to not even be allowed to feel that?

"Well, right now," Maud said, trying to lighten the mood, "I know I want to eat."

For a moment, Gretel's eyes widened.

Maud couldn't hold back her laugh. "Not you." She pointed to the kitchen. "There's plenty of normal food in there."

"Don't you think the witch will mind?"

"Witches look out for each other," Nuss said. "Unlike some people."

Maud managed to rustle up a loaf of twisted snail bread and peony jam, along with a steaming pot of frog scale tea (which Gretel looked very suspicious of, but finally said was not *entirely* disgusting). After the cold and terror of the day, it felt so relaxing to have a picnic in front of the fire— even if one of the other picnickers was a witch hunter.

Gretel leaned back, finishing her last bite of bread with a yawn.

And as soon as Gretel yawned, Maud found herself mirroring it. A warm drowsiness settled over her. It couldn't hurt to sleep for a little, safe inside this witch's cottage.

16
OKAY, SOME WITCHES EAT CHILDREN

Maud woke to the sound of clattering pots and pans. It was such a familiar noise—the soft rhythm of Agatha's kitchen in the morning as she prepared strawberry swirl bread or peppermint rabbit buns—that she thought for a moment she was home.

Then her eyes flickered open and she saw the witch hunter lying across from her on the rug. Grim was curled up next to Gretel, which Maud really felt was a betrayal.

Maud sat up to see the source of the noise: a witch bustling around the small kitchen. Maud jumped to her feet, hurriedly trying to flatten her hair. It always managed to look like a bird's nest after a good night's sleep, so she didn't like to think what the floor would've done to it.

"Um, hello," she said in her best polite-child voice. "I'm sorry, we didn't mean to barge in. We just needed some shelter."

The witch smiled at her over a bright yellow teakettle. "No problem at all, dear. My name's Mirtha, and I'm always happy to help a little witch in need."

Mirtha looked a little younger than Agatha, with wispy hair and such delicate features she could've been made of sugarpaste.

"And what's your name?" Mirtha prompted. "It's only polite to reciprocate."

"I'm Maud." She gestured toward Gretel still asleep on the hearth. "And that's—"

"Lovely," Mirtha said, busy with the kettle. "And what are you doing all alone in the Abandoned Forest?"

"It's a long story…" Outside the neat, square windows, Maud could see the rain had stopped. "Actually, we should probably get going."

"At least stay for tea, won't you?" Mirtha asked. "It's only polite, after all."

Answering for her, Maud's stomach gave a loud rumble.

She supposed it would be better not to venture back into the Shadelands on an empty stomach.

"I am quite hungry," she admitted with a small smile.

Mirtha poured something into one of the pots. "Excellent. It'll be ready soon."

Maud leaned her elbows on the counter, examining a jar of ink-black acorns. "I didn't know there were witches who lived in the Shadelands."

"There are a few of us." The contents of the pot bubbled. "Not many choose to live all the way out here. But needs must."

Maud shuddered. She couldn't imagine why anyone would choose to live here.

The kettle let out a high-pitched squeal as it came to the boil, and Gretel jerked awake. She leaped to her feet as if ready for combat.

"Feeling better?" Maud asked.

"Much," Gretel said with something close to a smile. Then she noticed Mirtha. She almost stumbled back into the fire. "Witch!"

Maud stepped toward her, shooting an apologetic look at Mirtha. "Don't worry, she wants to help us."

"She's a *witch*," Gretel hissed.

"Yes," Maud said, lowering her voice and hoping the witch didn't notice Gretel's rudeness. "And remember what we said about witches not all being evil?"

Gretel eyed Mirtha, suspicion still creasing her face.

"We'll just have something to eat, then—" Maud broke off. Then what? Gretel presumably wanted to go back to the Wolf Gard and back to earning her status as a full witch hunter. "Then we'll go," Maud finished a little weakly.

Gretel folded her arms, perhaps realizing the same thing. Or contemplating how to lead the Wolves back here.

Maud's heart skipped a beat. She hadn't thought of that, how she might have put this witch in danger. Maybe this really had been a terrible idea.

"Do sit down," Mirtha said, gesturing to the wooden table. "I'll just get the finishing touch." With another smile, she disappeared into a larder on the other side of the counter.

Maud went over to the table, swallowing her doubts.

"How do you know you can trust her?"

Nuss fixed Gretel with a glare. "How do we know we can trust *you*?"

Maud sighed, ignoring Nuss's interjection. "Like I said, *over and over*, because not everyone is out to get you."

"She seems too nice."

"Too nice, too mean," Maud said, sitting down. "No pleasing you."

Gretel pointed at the plates. "Why's she only laid two places?"

Maud was getting fed up with the questions. Hadn't she done enough to show Gretel witches weren't evil? "I don't know," she snapped. "Maybe she's not hungry."

Gretel *hmphed*. Instead of joining Maud, she went snooping around the room. To Maud's annoyance, Nuss hopped after her, nosing her way through some of the jars on the counter. Florian would be horrified.

"Don't do that," Maud whispered, realizing she did sound a little like the vulture now. But he wasn't here, so someone had to fill the role. "It's rude!"

Nuss's tail knocked over a jar of grasshopper salt and Maud hurried to clean it up.

Gretel held up a pastel recipe book. "'Recipes for Children,'" she read out, as if that proved something.

"Yes," Maud said, sweeping the last of the grasshopper salt back into the jar. "Good recipes to make *for* children."

Gretel leafed through it. "Then, explain this."

She pointed to a bookmarked recipe titled *Child-fingered Strudel*.

"That's just the name," Maud said. "Like how cheese rarebit sounds like it has rabbit in it, but it's only Gouda."

Before Gretel could complain again, Mirtha walked back into the room.

Maud's "I told you so" died on her lips.

Mirtha held up two wickedly sharp knives. "Who's ready to carve the meat?"

Gretel turned back to Maud. "And how about that?"

"All right," Maud conceded. "That looks bad."

Mirtha grinned, her teeth elongating to jagged spikes. Then she lunged for Gretel.

Gretel leaped back. Her hand reached for the sword that usually hung from her waist, but of course, it wasn't there.

Maud threw herself in front of Mirtha—perhaps not her best idea, but she still couldn't quite believe what she was seeing. She'd got strangely used to knives and weapons around the Wolves, but she never expected them from a witch.

"What're you doing?" Maud asked, ducking one of the gleaming blades. "You're meant to help a witch in need."

Mirtha snarled. "A witch, maybe." She sniffed the air. "But that one is a little Wolf."

Mirtha swiped again, and Maud backed away instinctively, stumbling into Gretel. Nuss jumped after them, knocking a pile of recipe books into Mirtha's path.

Mirtha kicked through them. "I'm only trying to help you, little witchling," she said with a not-at-all-reassuring smile. "How else will I feed you?"

"I'm really not that hungry," Maud squeaked, still backing away.

Mirtha's grin widened, teeth glinting. "If you'd side with the Wolves over your own kind, I suppose I'll have to eat you too. I don't get enough children out here. Your bones will make the most wonderful jam."

The witch swung the cleaving knife, and Maud dove under the kitchen table. The blade dug into the wood, giving her a moment to hurry out the other side while Mirtha tried to heave it free.

Gretel grabbed her arm, pulling her toward the door. "I don't think you're going to reason with her!"

Nuss hopped onto Maud's shoulder. "For once, I agree with the Wolf!"

Maud didn't bother arguing. She just launched herself at the door handle, trying to pull it open.

But it wouldn't budge.

"Is it magic?" Gretel asked.

If it was magic, didn't that mean Maud should be able to open it? She'd somehow managed that light spell to dispel the druden. But she couldn't feel even the slightest spark. Mirtha finally wrenched the cleaving knife free with an anguished screech.

"Duck!" Gretel yelled, pushing Maud out of the way.

The knife sank into the door, where Maud's head had been just moments before.

"Stay still, won't you?" Mirtha said in a singsong voice. Without a weapon, she held out her hand, fingers elongating to serrated claws. "It's not polite to make a mess before dinner."

One of those hands lunged for Maud, a single claw tearing through the fabric of her sleeve. Her clothes really weren't faring well on this journey.

"It's not very polite to eat people either!" Nuss squeaked, jumping over Mirtha's head to the counter and sending pots and pans flying.

That gave Maud an idea.

If Mirtha didn't like mess, then that's exactly what they'd give her. And she couldn't cook children with a messy kitchen.

Maud grasped the yellow kettle and upended it over the fallen recipe books.

Mirtha let out another screech, more incensed than ever. "Don't you dare—insolent child!"

Maud shoved at a pile of plates, sending them clattering to the ground.

"What're you doing?" Gretel asked, staring at Maud like she'd lost her mind.

"Can't cook us without any plates, can she?"

It was questionable logic, but Nuss immediately jumped to attention. "My time has come!" she cried.

The little squirrel flung a pile of saucepans at the neat windows.

"Stop!" Mirtha lunged after the fallen pots, momentarily forgetting her murderous intent. "Such rude children!"

Gretel grabbed a rolling pin from where it had fallen, brandishing it like a sword. She hurried over to Maud. "There has to be another way out of here!"

"I think there is," Maud said, pointing to the window. A

small crack ran through the glass where one of the sauce-pans had made contact.

Gretel didn't need to be told twice. She hurled the rolling pin with worryingly good aim. The glass shattered with a clattering smash.

Nuss swept a shelf of ingredients onto the floor with her tail, and the witch spun back to them with a screech, unable to decide which of them to scold first.

"Quick!" Maud yelled, scooping up Grim and sprinting toward the empty pane. She pulled herself up, covering the broken glass with her sleeve to make sure Grim didn't get any shards in his paws.

"Don't forget me," Nuss squeaked, grabbing on to one of Gretel's plaits as she passed. Gretel's eyes widened comically, but she didn't falter.

With an impressive leap, the witch hunter launched herself up to join Maud on the windowsill. They both jumped down, helping the creatures with them, and sprinted across the cobblestone path.

"That was very rude!" Mirtha shrieked through the window, fangs bared. Her clawed hands grasped the sill, ready to climb out after them.

"Faster!" Nuss yelled, as if Maud couldn't see the definitely evil witch running after them.

"What do you have to say now?" Gretel demanded.

"Is this really the time?"

Gretel glared.

"Fine," Maud conceded. "*This* witch is of the child-eating variety."

"When we're not running for our lives," Gretel panted, "I'm going to say 'I told you so' *so* many times."

17
WHERE THE
RUBY FISH LIVE

Maud finally came to a wheezing stop when they reached a silvery creek full of ruby-red fish. She couldn't hear the crashing footsteps of Mirtha—or anything else—following anymore.

"I think we lost her," Maud huffed, peering back into the trees.

Gretel pressed her hands to her knees, breathing hard. "I. Told. You. So. Witches *do* eat children."

"*That* witch eats children," Maud corrected. "And the Witching Guild wouldn't stand for it—" Maud paused, realization hitting "—which is why she lives out in the Shadelands."

"The Witching…what?"

"Nothing," Maud said quickly. She really needed to re-member she was talking to a Wolf.

"Don't worry," Gretel said. "I'm not going to steal your secrets."

Nuss wrinkled her nose. "I don't think the Guild would mind in this situation," she said. "That witch was mostly in-terested in eating *you*, because of the whole witch-hunter thing. Not children in general."

"So that makes it okay?"

Nuss primped her mousse fur, looking at her reflection in the silver water. "Yes."

Maud ignored them. She knelt in front of the creek. She wasn't sure it was the best idea to drink from a random stream in the Abandoned Forest, but she was too thirsty to care. It tasted surprisingly sweet and refreshing, like a gleaming crystal made liquid.

She sat back on her heels and looked up at Gretel, a twinge of disappointment in her chest. "I suppose you should get going back to the Wolf Gard now."

Gretel kicked at the ground. "I suppose so."

But she didn't leave.

"I was thinking…" she started.

"That's a nice change," Nuss piped up.

"I could help you," Gretel finished, tentative. "With whatever it is you're doing in the Shadelands. To help your mother."

Maud raised her eyebrows, momentarily too surprised to form words.

"I know you might not trust me—"

"For obvious reasons," Nuss interjected.

Maud stood up, wiping her hands on her trousers. "You don't want to go back to the Wolves?"

"I don't know." Gretel toed the ground again, not looking at Maud. "But I do know I'd like to try fix what I did. Well, what I almost did."

"So, you don't think I'm evil just because I do magic?"

Gretel shook her head. "Even if that witch *did* try to eat me...my parents also ordered us to bring you back dead or alive." Maud's eyes widened and Gretel hurried on, "So maybe magic isn't really the problem."

From a trainee Wolf, that was pretty revolutionary.

Maud knew Florian would say not to trust her. Agatha would probably remind her that she shouldn't talk to strangers. And Nuss had made her feelings very clear.

Grim did seem to have taken to Gretel, but Maud wasn't sure his opinion counted in this.

But, despite everything, Maud *did* trust her. She'd never had a friend before—well, one that wasn't made of gingerbread. But she felt like Gretel could be a friend.

Warmth spread through Maud, like butter melting slowly on a hot crumpet. Even standing in this dark and dangerous forest, with witch hunters and monsters on their heels, everything felt a little more possible with a friend at her side.

"All right," she said.

"All right?" Gretel repeated in surprise.

Maud nodded, ignoring Nuss's *harrumph*. The two girls grinned at each other. Maybe this could work, not fighting as witch and Wolf, but working together as friends.

"So how do we find this spellbook?" Gretel asked when Maud finished explaining. She'd half expected Gretel to balk at all the talk of witches and magic, but the reformed witch hunter seemed unfazed.

"I don't know," Maud admitted. "I had a map…"

"But it's back at the convoy."

Maud nodded.

Nuss hopped onto Maud's shoulder, looking pleased with herself. "It's a good thing you have me, isn't it?"

"Because setting fire to the forest is suddenly the answer?" Maud asked.

"No," Nuss replied, indignant. She pulled out a folded paper from the depths of Maud's hood. "Because I took a map from that witch's cottage."

Maud's mouth fell open. "You genius squirrel!" she cried, pulling Nuss into a crushing hug. "I take back every time I've said you're difficult."

She put Nuss down and spread out the map in front of them.

"Wait," Nuss said. "When am I ever difficult?"

"Can't imagine," Gretel muttered.

But Maud was too busy studying the map to respond. It was more detailed than the one Vira had given her, showing only the Abandoned Forest instead of all the Shadelands and beyond. In one corner, she saw a squiggly nest labeled *Night Raven Den*. That would've been helpful to know before. She traced her finger down, across a place called *The Swamp That Never Ends* (she was glad they hadn't stumbled into that) and over a ridge of trees that looked like a spine.

"Here." Maud pointed to a thin blue line labeled *Where the Ruby Fish Live*. "That must be where we are." She gestured to the bright red fish slipping through the crystal stream in front of them. "And I bet that—" she pointed to a spot on the map a little to the left "—is where the spellbook is buried."

Gretel leaned over to look. "How do you know?"

"Because it says 'danger, do not enter under any circumstances.'"

Nuss grinned. "Sounds fun."

The map took them along a jagged path that ran beside the creek. The ruby fish flitted along next to them until the rippling water ended in a clear pool, the fish darting in and out like bubbles. Beyond that, on the mud-slick bank of the creek, was a tangle of trees. It was framed by the wide pool on one side and a rocky outcrop on the other.

The wall of trees looked so tightly wound together that Maud wasn't sure how anything could get through—flesh and blood or not. Grim didn't like it. His ears flattened and he let out the closest he'd ever managed to a real growl.

"This must be it," Maud murmured.

Gretel pulled out her sword (which Maud didn't think

would be very useful when their adversaries were trees). "How do you know?"

Maud stepped toward the tight knot of branches. They were different from the gnarled trees that bent over the creek. She wasn't sure she could explain it. But there was something heavy and ancient about this place. And a slight tingle in her witchmark, as if it could sense the old magic of the glade waiting just beyond.

"I just do," she said.

Gretel cocked her head. "I wonder what else is in there. I guess this first witch wanted to keep it hidden for a reason."

Maud swallowed. She hadn't thought much beyond getting to the glade.

Nuss opened her mouth, presumably to supply some examples of monsters they were about to face. But at Maud's look, the squirrel seemed to think better of it.

Gretel didn't appear at all worried. She just hopped over the narrowest part of the stream and headed toward those strange trees. Maud hurried after her. She had to help Grim over the water—the wolf was sensibly unsure about all of this.

"Don't worry," Gretel said. "You'll have my sword."

"You can't come in with me."

Maud ran a hand over the nearest tree. It felt almost spongy—porous to the touch—and buzzing with magic.

"Why not?" Gretel asked.

Maud hadn't told her that part yet. Gretel might be a reformed witch hunter, but she was only very recently reformed. Revealing that Maud wasn't human, that she was gingerbread enchanted by a sort of magic that even the witches forbade, might be a step too far.

"Is it a witch thing? Because—" Gretel's words turned into a sudden scream.

Maud whipped around, her stomach lurching. "Gretel?"

One of the gnarled trees by the stream had come to life. Straining at its roots, it clutched Gretel in its spindled branches like monstrous fingers.

"The tree wants to eat me!" Gretel yelled.

Maud's mouth opened to say "trees don't eat people," when she realized something was wrong with this picture. Trees *didn't* eat people, not on their own. This wasn't the magic of the forest, quiet and ancient. This was a witch.

As soon as the thought hit her, a figure emerged from the shadows on the other side of the creek.

Maud squinted. Her mind was struggling to catch up

with what she was seeing. It didn't make any sense. But the woman was unmistakable.

Maud took a step forward. "Vira?"

18
WHAT YOU'RE MADE FOR

Vira picked her way toward Maud, stepping across the stream in a graceful leap and looking just as calm and poised as she had in the Bewitching Hollow.

Her green-painted lips curled into a smile. "Oh, thank goodness I found you." She put a hand under Maud's chin, checking her over. "Are you safe?"

Maud nodded numbly, too confused to form words.

Vira flicked a hand at Gretel, and the twigs tightened on her arms like claws. "And just in time to capture a Wolf cub."

Gretel stared at Maud, her expression slowly clouding

into a glare. "You tricked me," she said. "This was all just a ruse to get back at the Wolf Gard. You're—"

Vira twirled her fingers, and a vine coiled around Gretel's mouth to gag her.

"No," Maud said quickly. "That's not it—" But now she wasn't so sure what *it* was at all. She turned back to Vira. One problem at a time. "What are you doing here?"

"Your little bird found me," Vira said. "He was worried."

"Florian?" Nuss squeaked, at the same time Maud said, "Where is he?"

"In no fit state to travel, I'm afraid," Vira replied. "His wings were turning back into gingerbread."

"Already?" Maud and Nuss exchanged a horrified look. Maud had thought they had more time. She ran a quick hand over Nuss, surveying for any signs of gingerbread reversion. "But we haven't started to change back yet."

"Magic is different in the Shadelands," Vira replied. "It may take longer to catch up with you here."

"But we can still reverse it, can't we?" Maud asked, her voice cracking.

"Certainly," Vira said. "As soon as dear Agatha returns to her body, then her magic will tether them all to their forms again." She made a shooing motion toward the dark trees. "Just hurry up and fetch that spellbook, then we can save them all."

But Maud didn't move. Something felt off about all of this. Like there was a step missing in a recipe. Even Nuss looked unsure for once, nibbling at her paws.

"Not until you let Gretel go," Maud said, with a slight tremble.

Vira let out a tinkling laugh. "Why would I let a witch hunter go free?"

"She's not really a witch hunter." Maud glanced at Gretel. "Well, not yet. And she's helping me."

"Come now," Vira said with a tinge of impatience. "We can sort that out once you get the spellbook. You wouldn't want to let Agatha down, would you?"

That solidified Maud's resolve. She raised her chin. "I don't think Agatha would want me to abandon my friend." Her eyes flicked to Gretel on *friend*, a little hesitant. But Gretel's fierce glare urged her on.

Vira's placating smile vanished. "I don't think you have any idea what Agatha would want." She stalked forward, suddenly looking much less like a respected member of the Witching Guild and more like one of the creatures that prowled this forest.

"Did you know this is what Agatha made you for?"

Maud shrank back, her throat constricting. "What do you mean?" she stammered.

"You see," Vira said, "I've known dear Agatha for much longer than you have. We trained together. We shared the same interest in the First Witch and her spellbook."

Everything seemed to have gone very quiet around them, Vira's face filling Maud's whole vision.

"It didn't take long for us to learn about the glade where it was buried," Vira went on, "and the enchantments put in place by the First Witch. They aren't there to keep people out, just to ensure the *right* people can enter. A challenge to prove your worth. A riddle of sorts."

"'Nothing of flesh and blood may enter the glade,'" Vira recited. "'Yet only a witch may touch the spellbook.' Many have tried over the centuries. All have failed miserably. But we finally worked out the answer." Vira's face brightened with a smile that gave Maud no comfort. "You."

"Me?" Maud echoed. All this new information felt like it was hammering against the inside of her skull.

Gretel's face shifted into focus over Vira's shoulder, watching all of this with a confused frown. Maud hoped she was too far away to put all the pieces together.

Vira forged on. "All Agatha's other creatures were just experiments leading up to the grand finale. A creature not of flesh and blood, but with a witchmark." She leaned down, putting a gentle and definitely patronizing hand on Maud's shoulder. "This is what you were made for. Don't you want to fulfill your purpose?"

Maud felt very small. A tiny gingerbread person in the middle of a vast forest. The question that had always thrummed inside her had finally been answered.

And that answer was that Maud was a tool. A means to an end, nothing more.

"Well, run along now, dear," Vira pushed.

Maud shook her head. This was all too much. She needed a moment to think, to talk to Nuss, and—

Vira sighed. "I see we need more motivation."

She waved her fingers again. The leather cord around Maud's neck snapped, and the vial of Agatha's ashes flew into Vira's hand.

"No!" Maud yelled.

Nuss lunged after it, but a tree root coiled around her tail, holding her in place.

Vira took a delicate step toward the pool. She uncorked

the vial and held it over the silver water. One twitch of her hand would send the ashes into the stream.

"Now, let me be clear," Vira said. "Go and fetch that spellbook for me, or I will drop Agatha's ashes into the water. Then there will be no bringing her back."

Maud drew in a sharp breath. Would Vira really do that? She and Agatha had apparently been friends. But Maud could see a cold glint in Vira's eye that promised she would make good on the threat.

Maud looked at the strange tangle of trees. "How do you even know it'll work?"

Vira shrugged. "I suppose it is still an experiment. But if you get trapped in there for all eternity, I promise to honor your memory."

Before Maud had a chance to say anything—to even think anything—an arrow *thunked* into the tree above her head.

The tail of the arrow was carved into the shape of a wolf claw.

The Wolf Gard descended in a rushing wave.

Two grabbed Maud's arms while another Wolf snatched Nuss from the ground, sending hazelnut mousse flying. Across the clearing, another was trying to hack at the branches holding Gretel with little success.

Maud tried to pull free, eyes on Vira. "Don't drop the ashes! Don't let her drop them!" But in the clamoring chaos no one heard her—if anyone even cared.

The Grand Wolves advanced on Vira. The witch looked unbothered, an expression of vaguest annoyance on her face. Yet she still held the vial of ashes perilously close to the water.

Maud kicked at one of the Wolves holding her. "I have to get them back!" she yelled, her voice tearing.

But the Wolves were both taller than her—why was everyone taller than her?—not to mention stronger, and she had no spells to fight them off. Where was that flash of light from when she'd been hiding from the druden? She couldn't feel any hint of magic now. No great power beneath her skin that could help them.

From across the flurry of Wolves, Vira caught her eye. She fluttered her fingers with a curling smile. One that seemed to say "see you soon."

Then she whirled. In one swooping movement, she dodged Hieda's sword and grasped Gretel's arm. A dazzling blade of lightning crackled across the clearing. Maud blinked through bright spots it left dancing across her vision.

Vira, Gretel, and Agatha's ashes were all gone.

19
AN UNLIKELY
ALLY

The Wolves wouldn't listen to her.

Maud tried to tell them over and over again that Vira would be back—more prepared this time. That she would use Gretel again, and Maud had to find a way to stop her. She might as well have been talking to an almond croissant. Actually, she might've had more luck with the pastry.

The entire procession had set up by a trickling waterfall that must be the source for the ruby-fish creek. Determinedly not listening, Hansel marched her to the back of the convoy, to a cart she hadn't seen before. It was uncovered and empty—except for a metal stake and heavy chains fixed into the center.

The sight sent ice rushing through Maud's veins. She could guess what they were for.

Hieda and Ermen were waiting next to the cart with matching blank expressions. Maud wondered if their training had really drained all their emotions or if they were just very good at hiding them. Either way, it was disconcerting.

"You have to let me help," Maud said quickly. "I can—"

Hieda didn't even pause to listen before she hit Maud across the face. Maud stumbled back into Hansel, blood and pain bursting sharp in her mouth.

The Grand Wolf towered over her. "Where is our daughter?"

Maud's eyes smarted with tears. "I don't know, but—"

"Who is that witch you're working with?"

"Vira," Maud said. "But I'm not working—"

"What's she planning?"

"I *told* you," Maud said, frustration bubbling up. "She'll come back for me—"

Ermen's sharp eyebrows sank into a scowl. "Your threats don't scare us."

"It's not a threat." Maud exhaled heavily, the fight beginning to seep out of her. It didn't really matter what she said. They'd already made up their minds. In their eyes, she was a witch and nothing else. "I want to help," she finished quietly.

Hieda turned to Hansel. "Chain her up," she ordered. "Tell the novices they can take turns on guard. About time they did some real work."

Hansel nodded and dragged Maud to the cart, hoisting her up onto the platform with ease—it really was unfair that even the other children were bigger than her.

He clapped manacles onto her wrists, not looking at her.

"Don't you want to help your sister?" Maud pressed, appealing to the last person who might listen. "I know what Vira wants."

He ignored her. With a click, he locked the manacles tight, using a squiggly looking key. He jumped back down and handed the key to Hieda, who pocketed it.

Another Wolf threw a sack next to Maud. A sack that let out a very angry squeak followed by Grim's snuffling growl.

"Hey!" Maud yelped. "Careful!"

Predictably, the Wolf ignored her. But at least she had Nuss and Grim back, even if they were in a sack.

Hieda banged a hand on the side of the cart. "Maybe after a night out here, you'll answer our questions."

Maud wanted to scream that she was trying to answer their stupid questions, but she didn't waste her breath.

Hieda and the rest of the Wolf Gard receded to their fire, all the way at the front of the convoy, leaving Maud with only a pinprick of light in the darkness of the forest. Plus her two guards, Oskar and Falka. Maud might almost have been flattered that they thought she warranted two guards when she could barely do basic spells. But she wasn't convinced Falka and Oskar were competent enough for it to be a compliment.

Maud tried to move closer to the sack, but the chains were too tight.

"Nuss?" Maud whispered. "Grim? Are you all right?"

The sack emitted a muffled but irritated grunt. If Nuss could sound annoyed, then at least that meant she wasn't hurt.

"Quiet!" Oskar yelled, obviously enjoying his brief position of power.

Maud's shoulders slumped. Nuss and Grim were safe, for now, but that didn't make this situation any better. She was surrounded by enemies who'd like to see her burn. If

Maud couldn't get Agatha's ashes back—and figure out the spell—Nuss and all the other creations would soon be no more than swirls of sugar and gingerbread. And there was no knowing what Vira had done with Gretel, or what she might do if Maud didn't agree to her demands.

She'd never felt so helpless.

Her whole chest was tight, as if the chains were wrapped around her ribs too. She couldn't stop thinking about what Vira had said.

Maud couldn't imagine Agatha ever working with someone like Vira, let alone being friends with her. Then again, Maud had never imagined—even in her deepest fears—that Agatha had only made her as a means to an end. An answer to a riddle, no more.

But the more she thought about it, the more it made a painful kind of sense. That was the reason Agatha had always kept Maud hidden, had made sure she stayed away from the Witching Guild. That was why she'd given Maud a witchmark but then refused to teach her magic. Because she didn't need to know actual magic, she just needed to be able to hold the First Witch's spellbook.

Maud had always wanted to understand—to have some kind of reason for why Agatha had made her.

But now that she did, it made her feel emptier than ever. As if she might crumble at any moment.

She wasn't sure how long she sat there, curled in on herself, manacles clanking on her wrists. But it must've been long enough for Oskar to get bored.

"You know," he said, raising his voice pointedly so Maud could hear. "I think I should be the one who kills the witchling. I deserve to be a fully initiated Wolf."

"You couldn't even get Gretel out of those trees," Falka sneered. "What makes you think you could kill a witch?" She glanced over at Maud. "Even a tied-up one."

"*I'm* the one who was suspicious of her when she first joined the convoy."

"Maybe, but you didn't do anything about it."

"Neither did anyone else."

"That still doesn't give you credit," Falka said. "Anyway, I bet the Grand Wolves will give Gretel the honor. She's the one who tracked the witchling down in the forest."

"Nepotism," Oskar scoffed.

Maud squeezed her eyes shut. A wave of nausea coiled through her. How could they talk about it all so casually?

There was a shuffling sound, then the two novices got to their feet. Maud really hoped Oskar wasn't about to try to prove he could kill a witch, because she had no way to run.

But he didn't move toward her. "What're you doing here?" he asked, looking into the dark.

Fear jolted along Maud's spine. Was it Vira, back already?

But it was Ludo's soft voice that replied, "Shift change."

A tiny sliver of hope pierced through Maud, delicate as spun sugar. Maybe there was one person here who would still help her.

"I thought we had another hour," Falka said.

"They sent us over now," said another voice, this one making Maud's spun-sugar hope dissolve into nothing. Hansel.

"I think they wanted to debrief you on the mission," Ludo added.

With some disgruntled mumbling, Oskar and Falka made their way back to the front of the convoy.

"Don't worry!" Ludo called after them happily. "I'm sure you'll get some more chances to torment the witch!"

Their footsteps vanished into the distance, and Ludo pulled himself up onto the cart with a grin. "Didn't I sound convincingly bloodthirsty?"

"Uh, yes?" Maud said. "Very intimidating." Ludo looked

pleased with himself, but Maud couldn't relax yet. She might trust Ludo, but Hansel was out of the question. Where had he gone? Was Ludo planning on distracting him somehow? She hoped the plan didn't involve moss.

"What're you doing?" she whispered.

Ludo crouched next to her. "We're here to save you."

"We?"

"Yes," Hansel said, significantly less cheerfully than Ludo, as he jumped up to join them.

Maud narrowed her eyes at him. "And I'm supposed to believe that?"

"It's that or stay chained up here until the witch comes back."

He had a point. But Maud couldn't help thinking this was some sort of trick.

"He wants to help Gretel," Ludo assured her. Maud didn't think Gretel would be too pleased about that.

"And he knows the adults aren't always..." He shot a sidelong look at Hansel. "Reasonable," Ludo finished. Maud had a feeling that wasn't what he'd intended to say.

"We need to be quick," Hansel interrupted.

Maud shook the jangling chains. "Do you have the key?"

"No."

"No?" Maud repeated. "Then, how do you plan on getting these off?"

Hansel's throat bobbed, and he looked over at Ludo, hesitant. Ludo nodded encouragingly.

With a look of deep concentration, Hansel held a hand over the chains. He murmured something in a low undertone, and the metal glowed white-hot, then the manacles snapped open.

Maud gasped. She stared down at her now free wrists. Her mind couldn't quite line up what she was seeing with what she knew.

"You're..." she breathed. "You're a witch?"

"We don't have time," Hansel replied, not meeting her gaze. "They might come back and check at any moment."

"Come on," Ludo said. "We'll explain later."

Nuss let out an angry squeak along with a muffled, "Ahem!"

"Oh sorry!" Maud grabbed the sack, untying it to let the outraged squirrel burst free, followed by a forlorn-looking Grim.

"That was very rude," Nuss said, trying to smooth down her mousse fur. "Do they not care about my complexion?"

Maud smiled. There was something very comforting about Nuss being *Nuss*. "I don't think they do."

Hansel and Ludo's eyes were round as steamed buns, staring at Nuss.

Ludo reached out a hand, which Nuss slapped away. "What a fascinating specimen," he said in awe.

"I'm not a specimen," Nuss snapped, as if it was a terrible insult.

Maud cleared her throat, jerking the two boys out of their surprise. "The crushing time pressure," she reminded them.

"Yes," Hansel said. "Let's go."

They all clambered down, Nuss hopping onto Maud's shoulder.

To one side of the cart, they'd have to pass the glow of the moon-elk, in perilously close sight of the Wolves' fire. But the other way was blocked by the waterfall, so unless they felt like splashing and drawing even more attention, there was only one option.

Hansel peered around the edge of the cart, toward the distant glow of the fire, then gestured for the others to follow. Keeping low, Maud crept after him, wondering again if it was wise to trust a Wolf.

Maud trod carefully, using the soft light of the moon-elk to avoid roots and jagged stones. One of the creatures raised its glittering eyes to her as they got closer, still chewing slowly on dry grass.

"Careful not to spook them," Ludo whispered. "They're not used to strangers." He glanced at Nuss on Maud's shoulder. "Or talking squirrels."

Maud swallowed. It might've been good to know that *before* she was right next to them. She made a soft shushing noise to the moon-elk, like it was a soufflé she'd just taken out the oven.

When the moon-elk didn't dart away, Maud inched forward.

Crack!

Maud froze. She'd been so focused on the moon-elk, she'd forgotten to look at her feet. It was only a tiny noise, but it made the nearest moon-elk nicker, tossing its head. It set the rest of them off, all skittering backward.

"What was that?" a voice called.

"Hide!" Hansel hissed.

They were still too far to reach the trees without being spotted. The only cover was the watering trough. They dove behind it, pressing close to the ground.

"It's just the moon-elk," said another voice, almost covered by the crackling fire. "I'll check on them."

A dark figure moved away from the pale blue flames. Around the edge of the trough, Maud watched a pair of boots tramp toward them. Her heart was hammering so loudly now, she was sure the Wolves would be able to hear it.

The boots paused by the nearest moon-elk. "Something bothering you, girl?" the person murmured, patting it reassuringly on the back. Maud recognized that voice— and remembered all too well the sharp axe Rega carried.

Please don't look over here, Maud thought, wishing she knew how to do a concealing spell.

But the boots kept moving toward them. Maud pulled farther back, hardly daring to breathe.

Rega stepped behind the trough. Lantern held aloft, there was no way the woman couldn't see the three of them huddled there.

Everything seemed to still. The terrible moment solidifying as Rega looked down at them.

Maud glanced back at Hansel and Ludo, hoping they might be able to appeal to Rega—or at least come up with a convincing lie. But they looked just as frozen and scared as Maud felt.

"All clear, Rega?" someone called from the fire.

"Please," Maud mouthed. She remembered what Rega had said when they were foraging, about how not everyone who traveled with the Wolves was a hunter. She remembered the concern that had sounded so real in the woman's voice.

For a long moment, Rega held her gaze. Maud couldn't tell what the stern woman was thinking. If she'd turn on them just like everyone else.

Then, Rega winked.

It was so surprising Maud almost laughed out loud in relief.

"All clear," Rega yelled back. Without another look at the three of them, she turned away and her light retreated.

When it had faded away and the general chatter of the Wolves had resumed, Maud nudged the other two. "Let's go."

Without another sound, the three of them vanished into the trees.

20
AN UNWANTED WITCHMARK

"I brought some food," Ludo said an hour later when they'd found the shelter of a fallen trunk to rest beneath. He pulled out three wrapped pouches of hot stone bread.

Maud took one eagerly. Her meals had been far too irregular these past few days. She took a bite of the bread. It wasn't like anything she'd had before. Thin and crunchy but soft inside and peppered with pieces of dried grapes and herbs. She'd have to show Agatha this recipe.

If Maud somehow managed to fix all of this.

Ludo handed the other pouch to Hansel. "I know you like yours without chives."

"That's boring of you," Nuss said, and Maud had to agree. She added "likes bland food" to his list of sins.

Hansel shot a suspicious look at Nuss as he took the bread. He still didn't seem too sure about the squirrel.

"Do you eat?" Ludo asked Nuss.

Nuss folded her little arms. "Of course I do."

"Interesting," Ludo said, his fingers twitching like he wanted to take notes. "Where does it go, I wonder? Do you metabolize it? When you were made, did the witch have to sculpt organs too? An entire nervous system?"

Maud lifted Nuss and moved her away from Ludo before the squirrel said something rude.

"It's magic," Maud explained. "I'm not sure all your scientific rules apply."

"Magic and science aren't so different."

Maud thought of the Wolves' strange blue lamps made by combining different minerals and supposed he had a point.

She looked over at Hansel, who'd been very quiet ever since they left the camp.

"Are you going to tell me how a Wolf has magic?" she asked. "The rest of the Wolf Gard didn't seem ready to burn you at the stake."

"No one else knows," Ludo said.

"No one?" Maud asked in surprise. "Not even your parents? Or Gretel?"

Hansel shook his head. "No one."

"But…how?" Maud couldn't imagine hiding a secret like that for so long, especially from family.

Hansel folded his hands together. "My witchmark only appeared three years ago, when I was eleven. And I didn't tell anyone."

"Except me," Ludo supplied.

"That wasn't really by choice," Hansel said, but a smile tugged at his lips. "He wouldn't stop pestering."

Ludo knocked his shoulder against Hansel's. "You like my pestering."

But Maud couldn't follow the change in humor. "You kept it a secret all this time?"

Hansel's smile faded. "I didn't want it."

Maud stared at him. She'd spent her whole life eager for magic, desperate to be like Agatha. She'd never imagined there might be people out there who wouldn't want it.

"And how could I tell anyone?" he asked. "Just having a witchmark meant, at best, my parents would disown me. At worst…"

He trailed off, but he didn't need to finish for Maud to catch his meaning.

And she didn't have an answer for him. She'd seen how quickly the Wolves had turned on her. She wanted to believe the Grand Wolves would feel differently if it was their own child, but she could still see the cold fury in Hieda's face. It didn't seem like there was any room for understanding there.

"I taught myself what I could," Hansel went on. "Just to keep it under control, or for emergencies. Like with the druden."

"Oh," Maud said, the realization hitting her as she remembered that shining light. "*You* did that spell."

She should've known that she wouldn't be able to do something that powerful. It explained why she hadn't managed anything close to that since. But it still left a sour burn of disappointment in her stomach.

"I'm sorry I let you take the blame," Hansel said.

Maud shook her head. "I understand." She patted Grim on his soft ears. "And if you hadn't done the spell, I might've lost Grim."

She popped the last piece of bread into her mouth,

chewing slowly. "How will you explain this to your parents?"

Ludo and Hansel exchanged a worried glance. "Let's worry about getting Gretel back first," Hansel said. He looked up at Maud. "You said you know what the witch wants. Do you know how to stop her?"

As quickly as she could, Maud explained about Agatha and Vira, skimming over some of the more painful personal details.

"Now Vira has all the advantages," Maud finished heavily. "I'll have to do what she wants."

Ludo chewed his lip in thought. "Maybe not *all* the advantages."

Maud tilted her head at him.

"She doesn't know about us," Ludo said.

Maud didn't want to be rude, but somehow, she doubted that a witch hunter/occasional witch and a botanist would make much difference against someone as powerful as Vira.

"He's right," Hansel said. "The element of surprise can make all the difference in these situations."

"What're you thinking?" Maud asked.

"Can you lead us to Vira?"

She nodded. She was certain Vira would be heading back to the glade as soon as she could.

"But even with you two helping," Maud said tactfully, "how would we stop her?"

Ludo grinned. "How do you feel about the destructive potential of moss?"

21
MOSS, GINGERBREAD, AND OTHER DEADLY WEAPONS

Maud's palms were sweating with nerves when she stepped into the clearing again. It looked just as it had the day before. Or the night before. Or whatever time it was in this darkness. All signs of the scuffle with the Wolves had vanished. Even the wolf-claw arrow that had stuck into the tree above Maud's head was nowhere to be seen, as if the forest had wiped it all clean.

Maud stopped by the glittering creek. "Vira!" she yelled, her voice sounding much more confident than she felt. "Vira! I know you're here somewhere."

In a blink, Vira shimmered into view in the exact spot

Maud had last seen her, almost as if she'd never left. Gretel appeared, too, still held tight in the tree's grip, a snaking branch acting as a gag.

Any last dregs of Maud's confidence evaporated again at the ease of Vira's power. Maud couldn't even *imagine* spells like that.

"You escaped the Wolves," Vira said. Maud couldn't decide if the edge to her words was surprise or suspicion. "Well, that saves me some trouble at least."

Her eyes flicked around the clearing before landing back on Maud. "No squirrel friend today?"

Maud's throat was dry as flour, so she just shook her head. It was a huge effort not to let her gaze stray to Gretel or the shadow hidden in the trees that she knew was Ludo and said squirrel friend.

"Are you ready to be more cooperative now?" Vira asked.

Maud nodded, still not trusting her voice.

Vira swept her arms toward the thick darkness of the glade. "Go ahead, then."

Maud swallowed, keeping her eyes firmly on Vira. "What if it doesn't work?" she asked, hoping it didn't sound like she was stalling.

Vira shrugged. "Then I suppose you'll be trapped in

there for all eternity." She smiled, a smile that was all sharp lemon and sherbets. "But I promise I'll honor our bargain either way."

Maud scrambled for another question. "What if—"

Someone leaped from the trees. Maud tried to dodge but stumbled on the uneven ground. Hands grabbed her, pulling her upright. A wolf-claw dagger pressed into her side.

"I won't let you get away with this, witch!" Hansel yelled, his grip firm as he dragged Maud back toward the pool. "I won't let you get that book!"

Maud struggled, the knife digging painfully into her ribs.

Hansel leveled his gaze at Vira. "Let my sister go."

Vira raised her eyebrows, bemused. "You are in no position to bargain here, little Wolf cub."

Hansel's face twisted. "Fine," he snapped. "If I can't save Gretel, at least I'll take this one back to the Wolf Gard. I know you need her."

"Vira!" Maud yelled. She pretended to stamp on Hansel's foot, but her balance was off and she heard him let out a low *oof* of pain as her boot connected. She'd have to apologize later.

"Help!" she yelled again, with what she hoped was convincing fear.

"Don't come any closer," he warned Vira.

Vira's expression darkened. "You do not want to push me."

But Hansel kept pulling Maud back, away from all the others—past the tree they'd marked. Vira followed, giving Ludo and Nuss cover to start hacking at the branches holding Gretel captive.

"Don't try to fight me," Hansel said. Over Vira's shoulder, Maud saw Gretel roll her eyes at his theatrics.

Vira flicked her hand. *"Hsiuqniler,"* she hissed.

It felt like the invisible hand of a giant slammed into them. It knocked both of them to the ground with a jolt of pain. Hansel's knife flew from his grip and splashed into the creek.

Vira strode forward to examine Hansel where he'd fallen, now weaponless. Maud scrabbled back, as far out of the path of destruction as she could manage.

"Do you know what happens to wolf cubs who stray too far from the pack?" she asked, a nasty expression curling her features. "They get picked off. One..." She took another step forward. "By..." She twisted her hands together, preparing a spell. "One."

Before Vira could utter the words, Hansel threw his arms out. *"Tsug tsepmet!"*

Vira's eyes widened. She'd been expecting human weapons from Hansel and wasn't at all prepared for magic.

A gust of wind burst from Hansel's hands and lifted Vira off her feet. It sent her soaring backward into a thick patch of moss.

At the same moment, Ludo and Nuss finally broke through the branches holding Gretel. She leaped free and grabbed a spiky stick from the ground, running over to join Maud and Hansel.

She pointed the stick at Hansel as if it was a sword. "Did you just do magic?"

Maud wasn't sure if it was shock or horror that swept Gretel's features blank. Hansel just stared at her, his mouth pressed shut like he might be sick.

Vira's sharp eyes raked over them. "Working with Wolves?" she spat at Maud. "Despicable." Vira sank her hands into the moss to push herself upright. "But party tricks won't help you."

She tried to stand—but couldn't. She was stuck to the

patch of moss, her hands trapped and useless. The patch of moss they'd very carefully placed there.

"Ever heard of dragon moss?" Maud asked.

"It's used to trap prey," Ludo jumped in, always eager to explain. "With thousands of micro—"

Hansel put a gentle hand on his shoulder.

"Right," Ludo said, taking a step back. "Not the moment."

Vira glared at Maud. "Agatha would be so disappointed in you."

Maud tightened her fists. Maybe Maud didn't know what Agatha would say. Maybe she hadn't known Agatha as well as she'd thought. But Maud did know that if she had made any other choice today, she'd have been very disappointed in herself.

"I think Mother Agatha would have been proud," Nuss said, glowering down at Vira.

"Well," Vira said acidly. "You'll never speak to her again to find out."

On cue, Nuss scampered down Maud's arm and hopped onto the moss, too light for it to trap her. Maud didn't understand the science of it, but Ludo had been very certain. Something about surface areas and density. Maud still thought it was probably just because Nuss was made of magic.

The squirrel scrambled onto Vira's shoulder and snatched the vial of ashes from around her neck. She dashed back to Maud as Vira tried to grab her—but her hands were still stuck fast.

Some of the tension seeped out of Maud's muscles once she had the ashes back. Not quite Agatha, but a step closer to her.

Vira glared up at her. "You're very pleased with yourself, aren't you?"

Nuss puffed out her chest. "Yes, we—"

"Considering you're little more than enchanted dough," Vira finished, her poisonous stare on Maud. "A failed experiment. Do you really think Agatha cared for you all those years? She *needed* you. That was all."

Maud tried not to let her hands shake. To show how that cut all the way down to her crumbly core.

"What does she mean?" Gretel asked.

Vira's face split into a grin. "Your new friends don't know?"

Maud's throat stuck, as if she'd just swallowed too many gummy sweets. A sickly dread churned in her gut.

"Maud is not really human," she said, addressing the others. "She's not even a witch."

They were all staring, and Nuss was tugging on Maud's hair, but Maud still couldn't speak. No spell was holding her in place, just all her own worst fears.

"She's an abomination," Vira said. "A magical experiment made from banned, dark witchcraft and *gingerbread*." She spoke the word as if it was the worst insult. Her eyes flicked to Maud. "Do you know how Agatha finally got you right? How she figured out the answer to the First Witch's riddle?"

Maud took a step back, shaking her head. She didn't want to hear this.

"She took someone's final breath," Vira said with relish. "That's how you create the truest illusion of life. You steal it."

Maud's whole head was buzzing. That couldn't be true. Could it?

She'd always known she was more alive than Agatha's other creations. That she took on the form of flesh and bone, but she'd never questioned why. She'd certainly never imagined that her life could be a stolen one.

Everyone had gone very quiet. Maud was sure they were watching her, but she didn't know what to say.

"Did that ruin your new alliance with our mortal enemies?" Vira asked with mock sympathy. "Well, I have a little more bad news. You forgot the most important rule. Always watch a witch's hands."

Much too late, Maud realized Vira had used the distraction of her words to work one of her hands free from the moss.

"Emalf em gnirb!" Vira snarled.

A bright flare of green fire burst around Vira. Maud stumbled back, raising her hands to avoid the trailing sparks.

The flames ate through the moss in the blink of an eye, and Vira leaped to her feet.

Gretel tried to strike with her stick, but one of the hanging branches twisted around her arm and pulled her back. More trees sprang to life around them. Branched hands clamped around Hansel and Ludo. Another vine caught hold of Nuss, snaking on to curl around Grim's tail too.

A final flick, and the ashes soared from Maud's grip into Vira's outstretched hand.

Maud lunged after the vial with a strangled cry, but another spindled branch clamped around her waist.

Vira took her time. She smoothed her hair, adjusted her slightly askew collar and smudged lipstick.

"Now," Vira said, prowling forward. "Shall we try this again?"

Vira squeezed her hand into a tight fist, and the branches around the others squeezed too. *Crushing.* They let out gasps of pain, air being pushed from their lungs.

"Let them go!" Maud yelled, tugging desperately against the rough bark holding her in place. But it was no use.

"Of course," Vira said with a smile. "As soon as you fetch that spellbook for me."

"Don't!" Gretel shouted, her voice cut off as the branches constricted tighter.

Maud looked from her friends to Vira, her mind whirling. If only everything could pause for a moment, give her a breath to think. That's what Agatha always told her to do. But this wasn't a potion Maud had over-steeped or a cake that had gone lopsided. This needed more than a simple solution to fix it.

And Maud didn't have one.

"Do you doubt me?" Vira asked, and the others let out

choking breaths as the branches tightened again. "You really shouldn't question my nature. After all, I was strong enough to push dear Agatha into that oven."

Maud stared at her. "That was you?"

"Of course," Vira said. "I thought you'd figured that out already. After all, I only found her thanks to your attempted spell."

That spell felt like a long time ago now, the one that had ended in goblin guts all over the cottage. Was that why Agatha had never let Maud do magic? Because it might bring Vira to them?

The thought churned in Maud's stomach like bile. If that was true, then this was her fault. All her fault.

"I told her it wasn't fair of her not to share," Vira went on. "Not when we planned this together. But she disagreed."

"So you killed her."

"No," Vira said, as if it were obvious. "I left her ashes, didn't I? I just gave you some motivation."

Maud looked at the others again. Tears pricked at the edges of Ludo's eyes as he mouthed *no* and Hansel's face was slowly losing color. Gretel didn't seem to be able to speak, but her expression was imploring. Even Nuss was shaking her head.

They didn't want her to take this risk. To give the spell-book's power to Vira, even if it would save them. They were probably right; that would be the noble choice.

But Maud wasn't going to let anyone else lose their lives because of her.

"I'll do it."

Vira nodded slowly. She twirled her fingers and the branch holding Maud slithered free. "Hurry along now, dear. We wouldn't want your friends to run out of air."

Maud didn't look back at the others, refused to let her doubts clamor in again. She marched straight for the wall of tightly woven trees. She put a hand on the nearest trunk, feeling that oddly porous texture again.

She pushed against the surface of the tree. The bark gave beneath her fingers like chiffon sponge cake, drawing her in.

I suppose I am going to let the forest devour me after all, she thought.

With a deep breath, she stepped into the darkest part of the forest.

22
INTO THE GLADE

Maud blinked against the bright butter-yellow sunlight. After all that time in the darkness of the Shadelands, it hurt her eyes to stand in brilliant daylight. Once her vision adjusted, she saw the glade was beautiful. Shimmering shades of green accented by dancing butterflies that glowed with a soft rose light. Magnificent trees arched overhead, adorned with leaves as delicate as crystal. The very air tasted sweet and clear.

She couldn't feel a breeze, but something was sending the leaves fluttering. Or maybe these trees were more alive than most.

If the rest of the forest had felt ancient, this glade was something older. A small piece torn from the fabric of the world and frozen in time.

It felt like somewhere that ought not to be disturbed.

But Maud had to find that spellbook.

She glanced back at the strange trees she'd pushed through. She couldn't hear Vira's sharp voice anymore, but that didn't mean she had time to dawdle.

Maud took a step forward, closer to one of the towering trees, then recoiled with a sharp gasp.

There were faces in the trees. All frozen in utter terror, trapped beneath the bark, mouths contorted into screams. These weren't just sculptures. There was something unnervingly human about them—disconcertingly alive.

Maud guessed that was what happened to the people who failed.

Would that happen to her?

This place felt so peaceful, but with all this power pulsing through it…

She shook her head. She had to focus. Trying not to look at the frozen faces, she walked forward slowly. Each step was tentative, anticipating some kind of trap or illusion.

A tree sat in the very center of the glade, smaller than the others yet somehow more intimidating. Massive roots spread from it like spiraling veins, stretching out to every corner of the forest.

It sent a tingle through her witchmark.

As she got closer, she saw it wasn't just a tree. Close to the trunk, buried deep in the tangle of roots, was a gleaming stone.

Carefully, Maud picked her way toward it. It was so overgrown with moss and curling vines that she could only just make out letters carved underneath.

She knelt down to brush it clean, but as soon as her fingers touched the stone, the debris melted away like morning frost. The stone shuddered, and Maud scrambled back. It rose up out of the ground in a spiral—not just a marker, but a plinth.

This was more than a hiding place, Maud realized. It was a tomb. The First Witch had buried the spellbook with her.

Was it the spellbook that had created the Shadelands? Maud wondered. *Or had the Shadelands been created to keep the spellbook away from people?*

She leaned forward, trying to read the fading letters that wound around the plinth.

I settle where my roots have grown,
A place kept safe from flesh and bone.
Now this warning you must heed:
Do not dare enter for one's own greed.
Do not bend to the power you crave,
Or else this place will be your grave.

A chill crept along Maud's spine. It really didn't seem like the First Witch *wanted* her spellbook found. But what else could Maud do?

And, worse than that, where was it?

She couldn't see anywhere on the plinth it could be hidden. Vira had said it was buried somewhere in the glade, but Maud could hardly dig up this entire clearing.

She looked back at the twisting words. Vira seemed to think this whole thing was some kind of challenge, a riddle to be solved. So maybe there was a hint in there.

Maud read the words over again, murmuring under her breath. But they didn't make any more sense the second time—or the third. They just made her head spin. Almost like the language of magic itself. Something that shifted out of reach if she looked at it too closely.

Maybe there really was a part of witch training that involved learning how to be unnecessarily cryptic.

"I settle where my roots have grown…" Maud muttered. Something about that first line stuck out to her. The others each had a purpose, a warning or meaning. But that first line was almost unnecessary.

She frowned, looking down at the wide mess of roots the plinth had sprouted from. Maybe this poem wasn't written by the First Witch herself…but by the *book*. It sounded ridiculous, even as Maud thought it. But then again, she'd seen plenty of impossible things.

And if it was written by the spellbook itself, then that meant the *book* had settled where its roots had grown.

She knelt down, scrabbling at the thick roots that wound around the plinth's base. They wouldn't move—as solid as the stone above them. If anything was hidden beneath them, Maud had no idea how she'd get it.

Maybe this was where the importance of the witch-mark came in. Maybe she had to do some kind of magic to break the roots apart. But she didn't know any spells like that, and she doubted she could go back to Vira empty-handed and ask for more help.

No, it wasn't impossible. Maud had felt it all through

the Abandoned Forest, that thread of ancient magic tugging her on. *Helping* her.

Her other senses had tricked her more than once in the Shadelands, so maybe she had to rely on something else. The moments she'd listened to that underlying trickle of magic were the ones when the forest had truly helped her.

She closed her eyes and put her palms on the stone-like tree roots. She ignored everything else. The hammering of her heart, the fears nipping at her heels, even the faint rustle of leaves above her head.

In the darkness behind her lids, she couldn't see the magic, but she definitely felt it. A low sigh that rolled through the earth.

Her eyes flew open. The roots had pulled back to reveal a small crevice.

And there it was. Somehow much simpler looking than Maud had expected, just a worn leather cover with the single word *Witchery* stamped across it. Tree roots snaked around it, holding it in place.

She held her breath, staring down at the spellbook. This was the moment, then. To see if she could really touch it, to know if her witchmark was more than just a symbol on her arm.

She grasped the book, and the roots slithered away.

The leather was worn under her fingers and oddly warm, like sunlight was trapped in the pages. A choking laugh burst from her lips.

She *was* a witch. Enough of a witch to be able to touch this spellbook.

The relief at that thought died as Maud turned around. She had to take the book back to Vira. She looked down at it, her finger running over the rusted clasp. What power was contained in this that Vira wanted so badly?

Vira had said it held the spell to bring Agatha back, but Maud wasn't so sure now.

She looked up at the tangled trees that hid where Vira held the others captive. A new determination solidified inside her. Whether this spellbook contained answers or not, there were five very living beings out there who needed Maud's help.

She had only taken one step, when something tore through the earth at her feet.

She stumbled back, almost dropping the spellbook.

Something ripped itself from the ground, whirling roots and dirt, until it converged into the form of a witch. Maud tried to back away but crashed into another slowly co-alescing figure.

Five of them surrounded her, larger than life and all looking straight at her. One wore a pointed hat with a wide brim, another had a flowing tunic and long hair of trailing roots. One was almost entirely made of stone, their face an expressionless mask.

It wasn't just the First Witch who guarded the spell-book—it was her coven. They must've all chosen to stay trapped here for eternity, just to ensure no one else got this book. Immortal and immovable guardians of this glade.

No, Maud realized. They weren't guarding the spell-book. They were protecting it. Probably from people like Vira.

Maud swallowed hard. "I don't suppose you're here to escort me safely out?"

With a sound like tearing roots, weapons appeared in their hands.

She ran. Not that there was really anywhere *to* run. But still, she sprinted round the tree, hoping there might be another way out. There was no sign of more of those porous trees beyond. The sunlight melted into a thick darkness, as if the glade simply faded away into nothing.

Behind her, the strange witches were moving slowly, as if getting used to their new forms. Or maybe they knew they didn't have to bother running when they had her cornered.

Maud dove behind one of the tree roots, her heart thumping. She needed some kind of diversion, something to distract the witch spirits so she could get around them and back to that wall of trees.

But Vira had been very unhelpful in giving Maud anything to defend herself with.

She wished Nuss was here. The squirrel was always good for causing chaos.

But, again, Maud was alone. Alone and helpless.

She tore through her small leather pack. A lot of empty vials, a spattering of cinnamon powder (she doubted that would help against whatever these witches were), swamp slime, a few cobwebs, some flour, and the small gingerbread heart.

Maud gripped the little heart. She might feel alone here, but she wasn't really. Even without Nuss at her side, Maud could imagine what the squirrel might do.

Flour had a lot of surprising uses.

She and Nuss had experimented with it in the garden one day, not believing Florian when he told them the explosive risks. They'd blown a hole in the sugar-glass windows and almost set the rose bees' hive on fire.

All she'd need was a spark. The most basic cauldron spark, the spell every beginner witch should know.

A rock crashed above her, sending a shower of dirt and shards over her. The witch with the long, dark hair had reached her, and he was already preparing to throw another stone—this one bigger than Maud's head.

She rolled out of the way, the rock leaving a huge dent where she'd been only moments before. Tearing a small hole in the corner of the bag of flour, Maud ran again. Not away from them this time, but through them.

For once, being small was to her advantage. She dodged and weaved between them, using their heavy movements to confuse them, and leaving a trail of white powder streaking through the air behind her.

When the bag emptied with a last puff of flour, Maud vaulted into the tangle of tree roots again. Even though they were made of them, the witches seemed to find the roots harder to maneuver through. It should give her enough time to set off the spark.

But she'd need to run quickly as soon as she lit it or she'd be caught in the explosion too.

Looking down at her fingers, Maud tried to remember the spell. The ingredients were necessary for beginners, but a seasoned witch could do it from nothing. Maud wasn't a seasoned witch, but she was desperate.

"*Em rof thgirb ezalb,*" she murmured, trying to feel that spark inside her. The tiny kindling of magic.

But all she could find was fear. So much depended on this—on her. And she wasn't sure she could manage it.

"*Em rof thgirb ezalb,*" she said again, but the words felt insubstantial in her mouth. Barely solid enough to penetrate the air around her.

Maybe she was wrong. Maybe, despite everything, she just didn't have the power to be a witch.

Yes, she'd been able to touch the spellbook, but then these guardians had appeared. Did that mean she wasn't enough of a witch or had Vira just not known about the extra precautions?

A huge stone hand reached down and grabbed Maud's collar. It hoisted her up so her feet dangled in the air.

She kicked out, struggling to get free, but only achieved a sharp pain in her toe when her foot connected with the witch's solid stone arms.

"*Em...rof thgirb...ezalb*," Maud tried again, her voice hitching.

"Trespasser," the guardian hissed, and the others took up the call as well, as if the very glade were whispering. "*Imposter.*"

"No," Maud said, still straining to pull free. Maybe if she could rip the fabric of her collar, the guardian would lose their grip. "I'm meant to be here," she pressed. "I'm the..." Through the tangle of her racing heart, she tried to remember what Vira had said. "I'm the answer to the First Witch's riddle."

The stone guardian's features shifted, twigs and pebbles rearranging from cold emptiness to a deep frown.

Maud's fingers scrabbled against the witch's grip, but she might as well have been trying to move the earth. And the others were closing in now, their empty eyes all on her as they spoke in their strange unison.

"The book is not to be used for personal gain or power," the voices said. "We pledged our deaths to ensure its sanctity. We bound it in eternal darkness to protect it. Leave now, and we shall remain at peace."

But Maud couldn't just leave. Not without dooming her friends and Agatha.

"I don't even want the book for myself," Maud said desperately. "I just need to save my friends. Please…"

The stone witch guardian was unmoved. The others pressed in closer, and Maud felt their magic. It squeezed around her, brittle as lightning. But even in the presence of all that power, Maud couldn't seem to find her own.

A thought caught in her mind, a sudden memory. Why was it Agatha used gingerbread for her creations? It wasn't mere coincidence, it was a careful choice. Using gingerbread at their core made them better vessels for magic. Made *her* a better vessel.

So if there was magic around her, there was no reason she couldn't use it.

Maud didn't need Vira, or Agatha, or a spellbook to tell her she was a witch. She could feel it, as she always had, rooted in her bones.

Now she would prove it.

Digging deep inside, to that part of her that might be gingerbread crumbs but was also strong enough to have seen her through all of this, Maud said again, *"Em rof thgirb ezalb!"*

The words seemed to transform in the air, going from breath and thought to something weighty and real. A gleaming spark, green as the leaves above them. It leaped across the clearing.

The witch guardians hardly noticed. It was nothing compared to their strength, insignificant to them. But Maud only needed that tiny flicker.

Bracing herself, she tracked it through the air. As soon as it met the suspended flour, it blossomed from a spark into a raging inferno. It surged eagerly for the witches, for the trails of white powder Maud had left on them.

For a terrible moment, Maud thought it wouldn't work. That not even fire would deter them. But then it caught in a bright blaze, and the witch released her with an anguished cry.

Maud fell to the ground, clutching the spellbook tight to her chest. Ignoring the dull pain where her leg hit the tree, she scrambled to her feet.

The nearest guardian reached for her, hands clawing, even as the flames circled her. Maud ducked under her arm and raced back toward the entrance to the glade. The fire tore through the other guardians, severing the roots that held them together.

But the look on the stone guardian's face stuck with her. It wasn't anger that furrowed her features. It was sadness. They'd all chosen to trap their spirits here, to guard this spellbook for all eternity, without true peace. And Maud was ruining their sacrifice.

It sent a spike of guilt through her chest. She'd come into this tranquil glade and brought destruction.

"I'm sorry," she whispered. "But I have to take it."

Through the dancing flames and bursts of explosion, all the witch spirits were watching her with the same expression.

"Then, this shall be your responsibility, little witch," their strange, unified voices said.

They were right. It would be. But Nuss and Gretel and Florian and all the others were also her responsibility.

Maud turned away and hurried back to the tangled wall of trees. She couldn't let herself have second thoughts now, not when she was so close.

She passed the ghastly trees, all the previous trespassers caught in their bark. If only there was a way to trap Vira like that. But Maud didn't have that kind of power.

She only had the smallest spark, and that wouldn't stand a chance against Vira.

Her hand slipped into her pocket, grasping the small piece of gingerbread.

That was all she was. All she'd ever be. That was certainly all Vira saw her as.

Maud's fingers tightened around the gingerbread. A piece crumbled off under her grip.

She wouldn't give up now—wouldn't crumble. If giving the book to Vira was the only way to save her friends, then that's what Maud would do.

Common
Spells for
Uncommon
Witchery

23
THE VERY
FIRST SPELL

Returning to the thick darkness of the Shadelands made Maud briefly disoriented as her eyes adjusted again. She'd almost expected the witch spirits to come clawing after her through the trees, but they were just as trapped as everything else was in there.

The clearing looked the same as when she'd left. Perhaps a few more scratches on her friends' arms where they'd tried to break free and Vira must have sent more branches after them. But they were all still breathing—bruised and exhausted, but alive. That was what mattered.

Vira leaned against one of the trunks, examining her

nails. "You certainly took your time. Dallying risks your friends' lives, you know."

"You didn't mention the murderous guardians I'd have to escape."

Vira waved a hand. "Details, details," she said, as if it truly didn't matter. "Do you have the spellbook, or is it time for goodbyes?"

Maud held it up, still gripping it tightly. "I do."

Vira's lips parted a little, a look of wonder taking over her features as she stared at the book. So she really hadn't been sure if Maud would succeed.

Vira's relaxed posture vanished, replaced by an undeniable excitement. "Well," she prompted. "Hand it over."

Maud shook her head. "Not until you let them go."

Vira sighed. "Are we back to this again, dear? You are in no position to negotiate."

"How can I trust you'll stick to your word?"

"You'll have to believe in my honor."

Maud let out a laugh. Honor was certainly not a quality Vira possessed.

"Well," Vira said, "if that is not enough, then trust my determination." She clenched her hand into a fist, and all the branches squeezed.

Maud gritted her teeth. Two could play at that game.

"If you hurt them," Maud said. "I'll destroy the spellbook." She murmured the words under her breath, hoping that she could still catch hold of that spark as she had in the glade. To her relief, little kindlings of flame ignited in her fingers. She held them toward the delicate pages.

Vira's jaw twitched. "A nice little trick you've learned there. But it would only take a moment to kill all of your friends and take the spellbook anyway."

Maud swallowed, hoping her frantic heartbeat wasn't too obvious. "You could try to take it from me," she said. "But even with magic, you'd risk damaging the book. I'll set it on fire before you reach me, and some of these valuable spells will be gone forever."

Vira tilted her head. "You would really risk your friends' lives?"

"You're planning to kill us all anyway," Maud said. "I'm just trying to give us a head start." She shrugged, attempting to match Vira's calm. "And would *you* really risk the spellbook?"

Vira considered, the branches still constricting. Nuss let out a squeaking choke that made Maud's heart clench.

"Please, at least let Nuss go," Maud begged, her eyes on the tiny squirrel, almost entirely encased in vines.

Vira relaxed her hand and the branches mirrored her. A shrewd expression crossed her face. "How about this?" she said. "I let them all go, except the squirrel. Just to ensure you keep your word too."

Maud's mouth worked, her eyes darting between her friends. This was a huge risk to all of them, a gamble that might not pay off. But Maud knew she couldn't give up without a fight.

"All right," she said.

Vira splayed her fingers, and the trees dropped Ludo, Hansel, Gretel, and Grim unceremoniously to the ground. They were all gasping, Gretel rubbing at her throat where the thorned branch had been choking her.

Maud hurried over to them, careful to keep the sparks alight in her hand and still threatening the spellbook.

Vira threw up her palm, and the air solidified in front of Maud, forcing her to a halt. "No more dawdling."

Maud held her sparks closer to the pages, in warning. "Just let me confirm they're all right."

Vira rolled her eyes. "Sentimentality really is dull." But she didn't send out another wave of magic. Maud wasn't sure if

Vira agreed simply because she was fed up of discussions or because she knew that as soon as she had the spellbook, Maud and the others would all be at her mercy anyway.

Ludo was helping Hansel up, both unsteady on their legs. Maud hurried to Gretel's side, pulling her to her feet. She leaned in under the guise of checking one of Gretel's cuts. "Get to the other side of the creek," Maud whispered, as quiet as she could. "The others too. Trust me."

She knew *trust me* was a big ask, but there was no time to explain. She just had to hope Gretel would go with it.

Gretel looked at her for a moment, then she nodded.

Relief spread through Maud. At least they should be out of danger.

She turned back to Vira. The vines holding Nuss had morphed, lifting the squirrel to Vira's height. "Now," Vira said, her piercing eyes on Maud. "The book."

Maud moved toward her slowly. There was nothing between her and Vira, and, one way or another, the witch would get what she wanted. Maud was powerless to stop her.

"That's right," Vira crooned.

Standing this close, Maud could see where Agatha's ashes nestled against Vira's cloak, so close. Maud's hands were trembling so much now, she couldn't hold the sparks. She let them die with a sputter, her last leverage. Touching her finger lightly against something hidden in the well-worn pages, she held it out to Vira.

Vira took it with great reverence. As soon as her hands clamped on it, a wind tore through the clearing, biting and cold—almost alive. Vira's eyes were alight.

Maud took her chance. She leaped forward and pushed the book out of Vira's hands, at the same time snatching the ashes from around her neck. Vira dove for the book, giving Maud the chance to back away.

But not before Vira had righted herself, a new power coursing through her. The wind knocked Maud to the ground, pinning her in place.

"What use do you have for those?" Vira asked. "You couldn't hope to do the spell to bring her back." Her lips twisted. "Not that you will have the chance to try."

Gretel grabbed a branch, breaking it on her knee to give it a sharp end. She hurried forward, brandishing it at Vira.

"Stay there!" Maud yelled. "Don't come across the creek!"

Before Gretel had a chance to decide, Vira let out a hissing yell. She didn't need her hands to do magic now. Even her breath was power. A wall of magic swelled toward

Gretel, sharp and electric in the air. It consumed the grass as it rolled toward her, sure to devour Gretel, Hansel, and Ludo in an instant.

But the magic didn't reach them.

It crested against the edge of the creek, like a wave against a ship's hull. As if a barrier held it in place. Just as it had in the glade.

They all stared in astonishment, even the fierce wind momentarily ceasing in surprise.

"You!" Vira spun to face Maud, eyes wild. "What did you do?"

"I gave you the spellbook," Maud said innocently. "Like you asked."

The wind intensified again, pressing Maud back against the rough ground and stealing her words.

Vira opened the book and it fell to the page Maud had slipped something into. Crumbs scattered to the ground. "Gingerbread?" Vira spat.

"It was one of the first things Agatha taught me," Maud gasped. "Gingerbread is great for absorbing magic."

And with the amount of magic in that glade, even the small piece of gingerbread had been eager to draw it. The perfect vessel to transport all the protections of the glade until Maud had set them free again. Vira might be a witch, but she was also very much alive. And trapped.

Vira advanced on her, wind and magic whipping through her hair. "You little sneak."

"Details, details," Maud echoed, enjoying the expression of rage on Vira's face, even if it might be the last thing she ever saw.

This way, no one else would sacrifice their life for hers, and she wasn't letting Vira go free with the magic of the spellbook.

"Power is still power," Vira spat. "And I shall find a way out of here. I have all the time in the world."

She stepped forward, looming over Maud. "Unlike you." Magic pooled in her hand, bright as lightning. It solidified, lengthening into a sharp blade. Vira raised it high, a blinking star above Maud.

She braced for it to fall. At least her plan had worked. The others were all safe, and Vira couldn't hurt anyone else.

But a stone hand grasped the shard, magic dissipating around its fingers like smoke. The witch guardians stood around Vira, their expressions cold.

"*Trespasser,*" they all hissed in their eerie unison.

Vira squared her shoulders. "I earned this spellbook," she said. "You can't take it from me."

The witch with the pointed hat, topped off with a lop-sided toadstool, almost smiled.

In an odd mirror of Vira's own preferred trick, roots burst from the ground at Vira's feet. But they didn't just curl up her body, they consumed it. Bark crept across her skin like water slowly freezing.

Vira let out a screech of rage and threw a spell at the nearest of the guardians. But it was no use.

Maud was still trying to catch her breath, feeling oddly light after the hard pressure of the wind. She pulled herself up and crawled over to Nuss. The vines had almost covered the squirrel's face, but with Vira distracted, the spell wasn't so strong.

Maud tore at the vines, and Nuss tumbled free.

"Finally!" Nuss huffed.

Maud scooped her up, clenching Agatha's ashes tight in her other hand.

She backed away slowly, scared that she might draw the guardians' attention. But they didn't seem interested in her now, only in the person who had the spellbook. And Vira was too entangled in the consuming tree to notice anything else. She sent another spell at one of the other guardians and it faltered. But that did nothing to stop the tree bark.

Maud stared for a moment, too caught in her surprise to move.

She couldn't believe it had worked.

The others were all safe, and the creek now marked the barrier to the First Witch's glade. Vira was trapped here, bound by the very protections she'd told Maud about. And she and Nuss were free to leave, as they were not creatures of flesh and bone.

Nuss tugged on her hair, none too gently. "Maud!"

The squirrel was right. They might be safe for now, but Maud didn't want to hang around to find out what the guardians would do once they were finished with Vira.

Maud's toes had just reached the creek, mere breaths away from safety, when she glanced back. Vira's face was not contorted into fear like the other captured souls'. Hers was a mask of anger. One hand was still free, and her fingers curled.

In one last moment of spite, just as the tree bark consumed her, Vira flicked her hand at Maud. A final burst of magic sent Maud tumbling into the stream, and Agatha's ashes flying from her hand.

24
THE FIRST WITCH'S GIFT

Maud's scream tangled in her throat. She choked on water, her vision filled with bubbles and ruby fish. The water wasn't deep, but it was disorienting, and Maud couldn't seem to find her way to the surface.

Someone grabbed her and pulled her spluttering onto the bank.

"Maud?" Gretel said with a definite hint of worry. "Maud!"

Maud coughed and sat up. "I'm fine."

Next to them, Ludo hauled a very indignant Nuss out of the water.

Why had Vira done that? It seemed a waste of her last attempt at revenge.

Then Maud realized something was missing. The ashes. Vira hadn't been trying to hurt her at all. She'd been trying to hurt Agatha.

Maud rushed forward, throwing herself onto her stomach on the wet bank. The vial bobbed on the surface and she snatched it up.

But it was already too late. Water had seeped through the cork, tracking down the inside of the glass like tears.

Agatha's body couldn't be whole. There was no way to bring her back.

Maud sat back, panting as she stared at the vial. She'd been so careful all this time, and in the one moment when it mattered most she hadn't thought to save the ashes first.

Nuss came up to her, putting a hand on the vial. Her chocolate-button eyes were sad. The squirrel knew what it meant.

Not only was there no bringing Agatha back, but Maud and Nuss—and all the others—would turn back into gingerbread. After everything, Maud had still failed.

"What's wrong?" Ludo asked. "Didn't we win?"

Maud tried to smile. "We did. Vira won't be coming back." She held up the vial. "But neither will Agatha."

Gretel crouched down next to her. "There must be something we can do." She turned to Ludo. "Isn't there some scientific-plant way to draw moisture out?"

Maud shook her head. "The water destroys the ashes it touches. Even if we drew it out now, Agatha's body would not be whole."

"Uhh, Maud," Nuss said, clutching her ears.

Maud turned to ask what it was, then she saw. Nuss's ears were no longer soft mousse, alive and animated, but turning to brittle, overbaked gingerbread. The drain of Agatha's magic had finally reached them in the Shadelands.

Maud looked down at her own hands. A crack of gingerbread had fissured across her palm.

"No, no, no." It was too soon. She wasn't ready yet.

A strange sound broke through the air, almost like the noise the guardians had made when they first appeared. But softer, somehow, not a threat.

The tangled, porous trees on the other side of the creek were moving.

Maud's heart jolted. Had Vira found a way to break free?

But the trees didn't part. Instead, they twisted together

to form a face. Not one of the contorted, screaming ones, but the serene face of a young woman, her hair composed of suddenly blooming white flowers.

Maud's witchmark tingled, and she could see from the expression on Hansel's face that his had too. But it wasn't a malevolent magic. It felt somehow comforting, that same force Maud had imagined helping her throughout the forest.

She recognized it now as she had not then. The First Witch.

The face smiled. "Thank you for protecting my book."

Maud's cheeks burned. "I tried to steal it first."

"But then you returned it," the First Witch said. "And for that, I am grateful."

The branches moved again, beginning to sink back into the lifeless barrier.

"Wait!" Gretel yelled, to Maud's surprise.

The branches reformed, leaves quirked in a quizzical look.

"Can you help her with this?" Gretel asked, pointing to the ashes. Maud almost couldn't believe it. Gretel, of all people, was turning to magic for a solution. Wolves really could change.

"Of course," the First Witch said. "It is a simple spell."

"I thought it was only found in your spellbook," Maud said.

"No. You do not need my spellbook for that."

Maud let out a small sob. She should have known Vira was lying about that too. If Maud had never listened to her in the first place, none of this would have happened.

"Here, child." The First Witch's voice was soft, comforting as fresh-baked bread.

A golden glow emanated from the new wall of trees, enveloping Maud in a gentle warmth. The spell blossomed in her mind like a flower, almost as if she had always known it.

"It's too late," Maud said with a heavy sadness. "Her ashes have been drowned."

"There are other ways to create life, are there not?" the First Witch asked mildly. "As long as you still have a little of the person."

Maud's eyes widened. She looked from Nuss to her own hands. Yes, there certainly were. And who better to do that than them?

"What does she mean?" Gretel whispered.

"Gingerbread," Maud replied, which didn't seem like

enough explanation for Gretel but made perfect sense to her.

"How will we get back in time?" Nuss asked, pointing to her crumbling ears.

"I can help with that," the First Witch said, and a bright red mushroom pushed its way through the dark roots of a tree.

"A Toadstool Path!" Nuss and Maud cried together, to the others' utter confusion.

25
TO MAKE A GINGERBREAD PERSON

It took some convincing to get Hansel and Gretel to trust that the Toadstool Path wasn't designed to kill them and a *lot* of convincing to get Ludo to stop examining every aspect of it when they were running out of time.

The final mushroom—a soft pink dusted with white, like the cottage in the snow—took them right to the front gate.

The relief at seeing the cottage, warm and comforting and home, was eclipsed by its contents. Maud could see the rose bees, all turned back to marzipan, frozen around their hives. Sugar mice had lost their definition, no more than shaped sugar with strings for tails. The peppermint bunny was now hard candy instead of soft fluff.

And Florian.

He sat on the fence, as if he'd been waiting for them. He didn't cry out in greeting, though, or admonish them for all their ridiculous antics. He was just gingerbread, his black currant eyes empty.

Maud tried not to look at them. She would fix this.

She jumped over the fence, forgetting until they called after her that she had to let the others in through the protection spell. They all piled into the cottage, Ludo staring around in wonder, Hansel and Gretel looking a little more sheepish.

It hurt Maud to see the cottage. Not in its usual warm light, filled with chittering creatures and bubbling mixtures. It felt empty. Hollow as unfilled choux pastry.

"And the structural integrity," Ludo was saying. "It's remarkable how—"

Gretel cut across him, straight to business as always. "How can we help?"

Maud took a breath, steeling herself. She couldn't get distracted now.

"Now," she said. "We make gingerbread. A lot of gingerbread."

Gretel was a surprisingly good baker, Hansel was shockingly bad (somehow managing to burn the butter before it was even on the heat), and Ludo was very enthusiastic if easily distracted. In the end, it made for a good team.

Ludo helped Maud sculpt as realistic a body as they could, complete with organs and scientific accuracy, as Maud wasn't sure exactly what Agatha would need. Gretel took charge of baking times, making sure each piece was out and cooling and the next was in immediately. Nuss declared decoration her job, ordering Hansel around while refusing to let him do any of the work himself.

And Maud prepared the spell.

By the time they were done, it was dark, and Maud was covered in sweat and flour. A full-size replica of Agatha lay on the table in front of them, her gray hair created with careful spun sugar and buttercream, clothes arranged in delicate swathes of fondant and icing. Even her eyes were right, the exact shade Maud remembered, caught in sugar glass.

Maud stepped forward, apprehension simmering in her stomach. Now it was on her. She remembered the spell the First Witch had put into her mind—surprisingly simple but so important.

She pulled the ashes from her pocket and nestled them in Agatha's gingerbread chest, above the cinnamon swirl heart Ludo had assured them all was anatomically correct.

Maud held her hands over the figure. She closed her eyes, concentrating hard on that spark of magic. On channeling the power that swirled around her with purpose. The gingerbread was eager to absorb it, like Grim trying to tug a treat from her grasp. *"Em ot kcab emoc."*

She opened her eyes, looking down at gingerbread Agatha's face. Waiting for some sign that it had worked.

For a long, agonizing heartbeat, the gingerbread person remained as still and lifeless as the rest of the cottage.

Then a light sparked in those sugar-glass eyes. A glint that reminded Maud so fiercely of Agatha it hurt.

The light spread, shimmering down the gingerbread body. Her red licorice lips transformed into something more real, pulling into a smile. The result was not as neat as Maud, who was indistinguishable from a human, but it was very definitely Mother Agatha.

She sat up, and Maud threw her arms around her in such a tight hug she worried the gingerbread might crack.

She pulled away, tears pricking her eyes. "I'm so sorry," she said. "I ruined everything."

Agatha's new face creased into a familiar expression of concern. She even smelled like Agatha, of fresh spices and sugar.

"Oh, sweetest one," Agatha said, and her voice was just the same. "You didn't ruin anything. I should have told you the truth long ago. Then none of this would have happened."

Nuss let out a squeak, and Maud turned back to her, hoping to see the squirrel back to normal, all the creatures springing back to life.

But the gingerbread had spread, creeping down Nuss's snout.

Maud whirled back to Agatha. "Why aren't they all changing back?" she asked. "Shouldn't they be tethered to your magic again?"

"Oh, I don't think so," Agatha said. "I don't have magic anymore."

Maud stared at her, sure she must have misheard. "But I gave you a witchmark," she said. "We made you to be a witch again."

Agatha put a gentle hand on her cheek. "It doesn't work like that, sweetest one. My body was damaged. Even with this work you all did, there was something I would lose."

Maud's heart sank. "So we can't help them?"

"Of course we can," Agatha said. "You're a witch. We just have to tether them to you."

"Me?" Maud repeated. "But I don't really know any magic." She held up her already cracked palm. "And, look."

"We can fix all of that. You brought me back from the ashes," Agatha said. "You can certainly do this."

Maud was going to protest, but she stopped. Agatha was right. Maud could do this. She'd survived Wolves and night ravens; she'd traveled all the way into the heart of the Shadelands and come face-to-face with the First Witch.

No matter where her magic came from or how it worked, she was a witch. And she certainly wasn't going to let the creatures down.

"What do I have to do?"

Agatha helped prepare the ingredients, and Maud lit the cauldron spark, the spell coming easily to her now.

Gretel watched all of this in unreadable silence, while Hansel tried to stop Ludo asking questions every two minutes.

"The spell itself is simple," Agatha explained as she poured the potion into a small glass ball. "The important part comes from you."

Maud swallowed. That was more difficult.

Gretel elbowed her—maybe the closest the Wolf managed to affection. "You can do this."

Ludo and Hansel nodded in agreement, though Nuss looked irritable and Nuss-like as ever, even with her head turning to gingerbread. "I don't know if I believe in you," Nuss said. "But you better do this so I can fix my tail fluff."

That made Maud grin. She really wasn't alone in this.

She stood in the very center of the kitchen, holding a glass sphere tight in her hands, as Agatha had instructed. Agatha had said she needed to connect to the magic of the cottage, to tether it to herself and allow it to run free again. And to do that, she had to feel it.

So Maud tried. Just as she had all those days ago with the cauldron spark, she reached for the fleeting grip of magic. It was more familiar now. Not as sharp and powerful as in the First Witch's glade, but ever present and nudging, like Grim.

And she felt the way it connected through the cottage. Where it had absorbed into gingerbread and taken root, where it flowed off into the air. Letting out a breath, Maud prodded at the cracks, the places where magic was leaking out.

It bent to her command, manipulating beneath her touch like dough as she carefully patched it up and drew it in toward herself.

In a beautiful flash of warmth accompanied by the sharp scent of ginger, the cottage came back to life around them.

26
A DIFFERENT KIND OF MAGIC

That evening, once the creatures had all been reassured and the cottage had been restored to normal, Maud and Agatha sat in front of the fire. Ludo and Hansel were outside sampling some of the plants (Ludo was amazed that they were somehow both plants and sweets) while Gretel was sleeping off another cureall to heal her cuts and bruises. Florian was back to his usual self, dozing peacefully on his perch after finally finishing his lecture to Maud on why she shouldn't have left him behind.

Maud clutched a warm mug of peppermint cocoa in her hands, but she wasn't drinking it.

This was the first moment she'd been alone with Agatha, and she suddenly didn't know what to say. There were too many questions, and Maud wasn't sure she wanted the answers.

Agatha took a sip of her own hot cocoa, watching Maud over the rim of the mug. "You have something you want to ask me."

As always, Agatha could read everything Maud was thinking.

Maud put her drink down, and two marshmallow seals immediately jumped in, enjoying the warmth.

"Vira…" Maud started, and then it all came pouring out. "Vira said you made me to get the First Witch's spellbook. That you took someone's final breath to solve the riddle."

Agatha sat back in her chair. "I think I should start from the beginning."

Maud blinked, her eyes suddenly smarting. That wasn't a denial.

"I met Vira when we were both apprentices in the Witching Guild," Agatha began. "I was young and arrogant and believed that I could be the most powerful witch the woods had ever seen. That was how I became friends with Vira. We were both fascinated with the power of the First Witch."

Maud couldn't imagine that—for Vira yes, but not for Agatha.

"When we graduated, we used our new freedom from school to find any way possible to get the spellbook. That's how we found the riddle and why I began experimenting with gingerbread."

Maud's stomach twisted. This was too similar to Vira's story, and she didn't want to believe that was possible.

"We were getting closer," Agatha went on. "And I realized the only way to truly create life would be to use someone's final breath."

"To steal it," Maud said, her voice cracking.

Agatha nodded. "Vira was eager to try, but I was less… certain. And then…" She broke off, her gaze suddenly very far away.

"Then what?"

She looked back at Maud, a sad smile on her face. "Then I fell in love."

Maud blinked at her. That wasn't at all what she had been expecting.

"Her name was Rosenne," Agatha said, still lost in memory. "And she always saw a better me than I did. She saw the potential for beauty in things I'd only ever believed could be tools. She made me see the world a different way."

Agatha's expression clouded over. "But I knew Vira would not relent. So we went into hiding, in a house much like this, on the other side of the Frozen Waterfall."

"But Vira found you."

Agatha nodded. "She did." A flash of pain crossed her face, but she pressed on. "And she poisoned my beloved Rosenne with a venom that was steeped in cauldron water to destroy even her ashes. As she was dying, Rosenne told me to take her final breath. She knew what I could do with it."

Maud frowned. "She wanted you to get the spellbook?"

"No, sweetest one," Agatha said. "She knew that her final breath could create life. She wanted us to have a child."

Agatha looked at Maud, and the pieces began to fall into place.

"Me," Maud said.

"Yes," Agatha replied. "A daughter made by our love, from my gingerbread creation and Rosenne's life."

"She gave her life for mine?" Maud asked, her voice small.

"In a way." Agatha nodded. "She was always braver than

me. She would never have lived her life in hiding." Agatha folded her hands in her lap, taking a breath before she finished the story. "That's why I didn't want you learning magic. I knew if you did a spell, Vira would sense it. She knew my creations too well. And when she came that day, I didn't want you anywhere near her. And, well…" Agatha nodded to Maud. "You know what happened next."

Maud's throat was stuck, salty tears trickling down her cheeks. "Why didn't you ever tell me about Rosenne?"

Agatha looked down at her clasped fingers. "I'm sorry. I should have. But it was too painful, and I didn't want to do anything that might lead Vira to us. Keeping it all a secret seemed like the safest choice."

Maud stared into the fire. She supposed she did understand that. The same way she understood why Hansel had never told anyone about his witchmark or why she'd lied when she first found herself in the Wolves' convoy.

She looked back up at Agatha. "What was she like?"

Agatha's face broke into a smile. "Very much like you."

"Was she a witch?"

"She was," Agatha said. "And I think that's why I wanted to make you a witch. To honor her memory. Some of the spells in my book are hers."

"Oh no," Maud said, her eyes widening in horror as she remembered. "I lost your spellbook! So much happened, and the Wolves—"

Agatha took her hands in hers. "Don't worry," she said. "I remember all the spells. We can make a new spellbook, one we work on together."

"You mean…" Maud said slowly. "You mean you'll teach me magic?"

"If I cannot do the spells anymore, they have to find some way to live on." Agatha's eyes glittered. "I can think of no better way than through you."

Maud smiled. There was still so much she wanted to know about all of this, about Rosenne and who she'd been. About what Maud's life would look like now, without the threat of Vira. What her new friends would do, now everything had changed.

But for this moment, Maud felt content, warm and safe in the comfort of the gingerbread cottage. Certain of the fact that even if she was made of gingerbread, even if she had been made and not born, she was still a witch.

And she would learn to be a great one.

* * * * *

ACKNOWLEDGMENTS

Somehow writing acknowledgments is harder than writing the whole rest of the book! So many people played a part in making *The Gingerbread Witch* a real book, and I want to make sure I thank them all properly.

First I have to thank my wonderful editor, Connolly Bottum, who loved this book from the beginning and believed in it before I did. Your amazing work, notes, and ideas for this book have truly been invaluable. Thank you as well to everyone else at Inkyard Press: Bess Braswell, Brittany Mitchell, and Laura Gianino. Huge thank you to Jerri Gallagher, copyeditor extraordinaire. Thank you to Petur Antonsson for the absolutely stunning cover illustration (you brought the characters to life so perfectly!) and to Neil Swaab for the wonderful art direction.

Thank you to my lovely agent, Patrice Caldwell, and all the brilliant people at New Leaf Literary: especially Meredith, Suzie, and Jo, I really appreciate your help with everything! And thank you to all the other amazing publishing people who had a hand in this book: Natascha Morris, Naomi Davies, James McGowan, and the team at Book-Ends.

Thank you to all my writing friends and every person who is part of this writing community. You are truly all magical. Special thank you, as ever, to Katie Passerotti for your unwavering help and support with all my writing— but especially for my incessant questions on line edits. Edria and Nuss will definitely be best friends forever. To Tara Gilbert, the most supportive and kind friend I could ask for, I don't know what I'd do without you. Huge thank-yous to Tiffany Elmer who continues to be the best dragon mom, to my partner in crime/long-time nemesis, Briston Brooks, and to my debut buddy and publishing friend for life, Zabé Ellor.

Thanks as well to Tamara Mahmood Hayes for all the sprints, to Kalyn Josephson for taking this middle grade debut journey with me, and Kianna Shore for all the food-related puns. Eternal gratitude (not enough synonyms for my thanks!) to more lovely writing friends: Delara Adams, Sarah Williams, Rosey Waters, Kindra Pring, Katie Hahn, V Walker, Tiffany Meuret, and Colleen Mulhall. And to all my hatchlings: I love you and I'm so glad I got to put a dragon hatchling in this book!

Thank you to all the fantastic librarians, booksellers, bloggers, bookstagrammers, and other bookish people who have championed both this book and my debut. Especially in the current times, having that support has meant the world to me, and I honestly can't thank you all enough!

A huge thank-you to all my friends who have to deal with me constantly saying "I can't, I have a deadline": Allie, Marisa, Elo, Peyton, Anayib, Francesca, and Gabrielle. You're all amazing and I couldn't do this without you. Thank you as always to Christa Fassi for being the best coach and support. Thank you as well to Geo and Isabel for the in-depth discussions on tiny line edits! I appreciate you ignoring your dinner for them. Special thank-you to Lila Victor, the number one self-appointed publicist and bookmark put-together-er (can you tell I'm running out of descriptors now?).

Thank you, as always, to my wonderful family, without whom none of this would have been possible. To my mum for her endless and amazing support. To my sister Clemmie for always being a poophead (yes, I managed to get that in this book too). To my dad for fostering my love of writing. To my aunt Jann for all her help and guidance. Thank you especially to Becky, who was the first person I let read my writing, and Emma, who always gave me books I adored (and Jonny for putting up with me). And, of course, to my grandparents, who this book is dedicated to. And for the rest of my extensive, far-too-big-to-list-here family: thank you all for your love and support.

The final thank-you in this one goes to Tiny, the sweetest cat. You didn't get to see this published, but I'll never forget how you helped me write "The End."